I0610963

FLIRT AWAY

ZANE'S STORY

THE EMERALD CITY SERIES
BOOK FOUR

JEN TALTY

JUPITER PRESS

This book is a work of fiction. Names, characters, places, and incidents are products of the author's imagination or used fictitiously. Any resemblance to actual events or locales or persons living or dead is entirely coincidental.

Copyright © 2021 by Jen Talty All rights reserved.

No part of this work may be used, stored, reproduced or transmitted without written permission from the publisher except for brief quotations for review purposes as permitted by law. This book is licensed for your personal enjoyment only. This book may not be re-sold or given away to other people. If you would like to share this book with another person, please purchase an additional copy for each recipient. If you're reading this book and did not purchase it, or it was not purchased for your use only, please purchase your own copy.

Originally published by Lady Boss Press.

PRAISE FOR JEN TALTY

"Deadly Secrets is the best of romance and suspense in one hot read!" *NYT Bestselling Author Jennifer Probst*

"A charming setting and a steamy couple heat up the pages in a suspenseful story I couldn't put down!" *NY Times and USA today Bestselling Author Donna Grant*

"Jen Talty's books will grab your attention and pull you into a world of relatable characters, strong personalities, humor, and believable storylines. You'll laugh, you'll cry, and you'll rush to get the next book she releases!" Natalie Ann USA Today Bestselling Author

"I positively loved *In Two Weeks*, and highly recommend it. The writing is wonderful, the story is fantastic, and the characters will keep you coming back for more. I can't wait to get my hands on future installments of the NYS Troopers series." *Long and Short Reviews*

"*In Two Weeks* hooks the reader from page one. This is a fast paced story where the development of the romance grabs you emotionally and the suspense keeps you sitting on the edge of your chair. Great characters, great writing, and a believable plot that can be a warning to all of us." *Desiree Holt, USA Today Bestseller*

"*Dark Water* delivers an engaging portrait of wounded hearts as the memorable characters take you on a healing journey of love. A mysterious death brings danger and intrigue into the drama, while sultry passions brew into a believable plot that melts the reader's heart. Jen Talty pens an entertaining romance that grips the heart as the colorful and dangerous story unfolds into a chilling ending." *Night Owl Reviews*

"This is not the typical love story, nor is it the typical mystery. The characters are well rounded and interesting." *You Gotta Read Reviews*

"Murder in Paradise Bay is a fast-paced romantic thriller with plenty of twists and turns to keep you guessing until the end. You won't want to miss this one..." *USA Today bestselling author Janice Maynard*

FLIRT AWAY

AN EMERALD CITY SERIES NOVELLA

Zane's Story

USA Today Bestseller
JEN TALTY

By day, Dixie Gaynor spends her time helping couples work through their relationship issues. By night, she writes a blog: Create the Dew, dedicated to helping women find their sexual groove. Unfortunately, Dixie feels like a fraud and decides she needs to take a walk on the wild side—or at least as wild as she's willing to go.

Zane Pierce has worked at Club Allure for the better part of five years. While he doesn't have the sexual tastes the club is notorious for, he does hope to find an open-minded, nonjudgmental woman willing to try new things—all while maintaining a modicum of privacy. Lucky for him, the stunning beauty who walks into the club appears to be exactly what he's looking for—until details of their sex life end up on the internet.

Will Zane be able to come to terms with his love life being a teaching tool, or will he let the only woman he's ever truly cared for walk right out of Club Allure?

And his life.

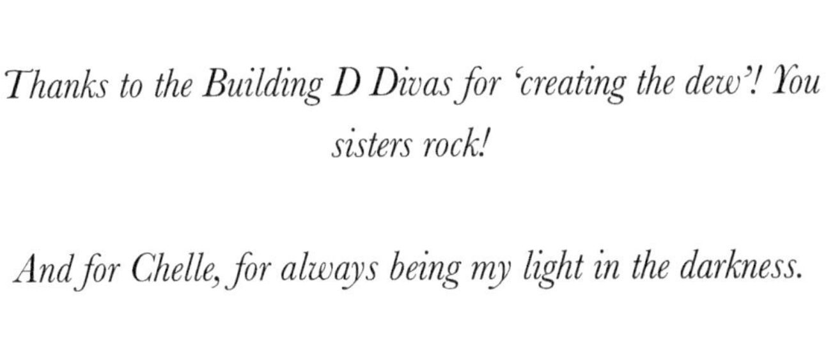

Thanks to the Building D Divas for 'creating the dew'! You sisters rock!

And for Chelle, for always being my light in the darkness.

Zane leaned against the railing and inhaled the salty air. Birds flew over the massive yacht where his cousin and her new husband had tied the knot. It had been a beautiful ceremony and Zane couldn't be happier for the couple. They had been through so much to find each other again and they deserved some smooth sailing.

He tilted his chin, closed his eyes, and let the rarity of the sun blazing in a blue sky warm his face. Only Darcie could summon such a spectacular day on the Puget Sound.

"Watch ya doing, cuz?" the sound of Darcie's voice startled him. His champagne sloshed over the rim of the flute and landed on the side of his hand.

"Shit. You scared me." He licked the side of his hand and took a hearty swig.

Darcie smiled, resting her hands on her baby bump. "You've been unusually quiet the past few weeks."

He jerked his head. "You've been a little busy getting married."

"That's true, but it doesn't change the fact that you and I haven't been communicating like usual. I know it's been sucky ever since you and what's-her-face broke up."

He chuckled. "She has a name. It's Zoe."

"I never liked her." Darcie lowered her chin. "No one does. Including Xavier and don't get me going on what your parents think of her. Besides, since that whole kerfuffle with you, Rebecca, and Erik, you haven't been the same."

Zane reached behind his head and undid his bun. He ran his hand through his thick, wavy hair before securing it back in place. The breakup with Zoe had been necessary, and he knew it, but that didn't mean it didn't still hurt. Zoe wanted him to quit his job. To leave Club Allure. He was sure he could find a new position somewhere else easily enough, but he enjoyed the people he worked with and he'd recently been promoted.

That meant something.

Zoe took it as he liked hanging around the sex club more than being with her, which wasn't true.

"Erik and I are in a good place. I'm truly happy for him," Zane said.

Darcie reached out and squeezed his biceps. "I know. I watched your heart break, and I saw how you came back from it. You're a good man with a wonderful soul, but you have shit taste in the people you date these days." She lowered her chin. "Both genders included."

He laughed. Most of his family had come to accept his sexuality, though some still held on to their judgments but didn't voice them to him directly. Darcie, however, had always supported him no matter what. Same with her siblings as well as her parents. Growing up, Zane spent a lot of time with his favorite aunt and uncle. He and Darcie were about the same age and often got in their fair share of trouble as kids. "I've been a little gun-shy since Rebecca."

"She's a bitch and a half."

Zane wasn't one for name-calling, but he wasn't about to defend Rebecca with his family. What she had done was unforgivable. But it was in the past and he didn't want to live there anymore. He wanted to find someone who rocked his world the same way Reid had turned Darcie's upside down and sideways. They were so in love it was almost disgusting, and he thought Jag and Callie were bad. "I don't want what happened to rule my life anymore."

Crystal Morning, a close family friend, strolled across the deck with a smile on her face and two cupcakes in each hand. "What are we talking about?"

"Zane's love life." Darcie snagged one of the tasty treats and immediately dug in.

"Last I heard, he didn't have one." Crystal shoved the sugary cake under his nose.

"Thanks." How could he refuse the best baker in all of Seattle? He'd gotten used to seeing people he knew in and out of Club Allure. At first, it made him blush to see some of his friends or random people he'd known, like Crystal and her cop husband, at Allure. It only affected him because he didn't have the sexual appetite for what the club offered, but he respected those who did and what Allure had to offer. He, of all people, certainly didn't judge, especially when it was his brother who had helped him get the job.

"Are we looking to fix Zane up? Because I know

a few women who would be perfect." Crystal rested her forearms over the railing and stared out over Puget Sound. Her hair caught the wind and blew over her shoulders.

"No. I'm good," Zane said quickly.

"Oh. I think you should absolutely set him up." Darcie poked him in the shoulder. "And when she does, you need to accept. It's not like you've been able to pick the right person, so why not let someone else give it a go."

"Maybe I like being single." Zane arched a brow.

"And maybe I'm not utterly terrified of being a mother." Darcie patted her belly. "I will probably drop this kid on his head."

"Hey, Troy dropped you on yours, and you turned out okay." Zane had always loved spending time with his cousins. He loved his brother and his parents. He had a great relationship with them; they were as thick as thieves. However, the Bowie side of the family always seemed a bit more his style.

"Let's stay focused here," Crystal said. "If I find you a date, will you promise me to go out with him or her?"

Zane thought about it for a moment. He

couldn't say that he was lonely. His life was full. He loved his job. He had his family and good friends.

However, he wasn't opposed to dating—the right person. "All right. I'll do it."

*D*ixie Gaynor closed her eyes and inhaled sharply, the rich scent of chocolate and vanilla assaulting her nose. "Oh, my God, Crystal. I almost don't want to take a bite."

Crystal Morning laughed. "You've got a full box, so don't be shy."

With her pinky stuck up into the air as if she were a total snob, Dixie took what her mother would call *a ladylike nibble*. Which meant she barely allowed the frosting into her mouth, let alone the tasty treat.

"Seriously? I have half a mind to stuff that cupcake right in your face."

And that right there was why Dixie loved Crystal so much. Of all her friends, Crystal never made her feel like the extra pounds she carried were anything to be ashamed of—or that they defined her as a person or a woman. As a matter of fact, Crystal had never said a single word to her about her weight unless Dixie brought it up. Not once.

Not something Dixie could say about most of her friends, and certainly not her family.

Especially her size-four mother—the plastic surgeon specializing in making women look and feel beautiful.

On the outside.

As if a nip and a tuck could cure life's problems.

A group of young ladies strolled by, wearing tight leggings that showed off their toned legs. And, of course, formfitting tops that left nothing to the imagination. None of them had a single roll.

Even their boobs were nice, tight, and lifted toward the sky.

Probably fake, but not the point.

Dixie sighed. The old tapes constantly played in her mind, and she couldn't stop them, though not for lack of trying. She resented that she couldn't pause them or even erase them because they occasionally controlled not only her thinking, but her actions.

"If I eat more than half of this now, I'll be on

my third by dinner." She wiped her fingers with a napkin and set the decadent treat back inside the box. She'd ordered the cupcakes to share with her clients, something she did a couple of times a month. And she always treated herself to a few. But she had to be careful. She understood how her mind and stomach worked and they were often in opposition.

It wasn't as if she ate like this regularly. But she *did* like her food, and she made no apologies for having an appetite. Most of the time she loved her body, and she loved herself.

But every once in a while, she allowed someone to tell her not to.

She'd come to embrace being plus-sized five years ago after hating herself for spending a year on a yo-yo diet, going between a size four and a size twelve. She'd landed on the other side of the sofa as a patient after making herself so anxious that she couldn't even eat food in front of people. When she did eat, it consisted of watermelon, salad, and maybe a few nuts. She was more unhealthy as a skinny person than she'd ever been as a fat one.

When she started eating again, she'd spent more time puking up what she put into her mouth than working on taking care of herself.

But those days were behind her. Why then did she sometimes feel so alone?

Because her mother repeatedly told her she needed a man and in order to get one, she needed to be thinner.

Worse, Dixie had let her mother get under her skin.

She raised the paper coffee mug to her lips and tasted the bitter caffeine rush. She stared out toward Puget Sound, watching the ferry leave the port. "I don't know if you read my blog or not, but I post about being a plus-sized woman."

"I love your blog, and I tell all my customers to read it." Crystal inched closer on the park bench and looped her arm around Dixie's shoulders. "The pictures are amazing. You look beautiful."

"Thanks." Dixie fiddled with the cup and let out a long breath. "Did you read the comments?"

"Don't even go there," Crystal said, giving her a good shake. "People are idiots."

"That's not even what sucks." Dixie shifted her gaze, staring her longtime friend in the eyes. "The pictures were filtered. I'm a fraud. I'm not living what I blog about, and that's being real." She shouldn't have let her mother or her sister see those images. "I have to either kill the blog or… or…"

She let her words trail off. The idea of telling the world she was the name behind *Create the Dew* terrified her because it meant she'd not only be exposing her true self, but she'd be forced to accept herself.

"What are you talking about? You are the most genuine person I know. And you've always said that haters are part of the blogging business. You're out there, helping women. Some of my friends have totally become stronger and more assertive, thanks to you. I think it's amazing."

"I'm telling women to be comfortable in their own skin and not to let men—or anyone else for that matter—control their perceptions of themselves, and yet I'm doing it." She shook her head, letting out a long breath. "I knew putting anything but a photo from the neck up would bring out the crazies who think women bigger than a size two don't have an active sex life, much less a good one. But then I went and put the photograph through a filter, smoothing out my hips and stomach, making me look like I'm at least two sizes smaller."

"Come on, we all do that."

"Do you?"

"Well, no," Crystal said. "But I know a lot of women who do."

Dixie wouldn't argue that point. She knew it

was true, but she should be better because of her profession. "Perhaps, but I'm single. And how many men are knocking down my door to date me?" She held up her hand. Right now, she didn't need one of her dear friends to tell her how beautiful she thought Dixie was. "Besides, I'm still anonymous. My blog isn't under my real name, and it's not connected to my work as a relationship therapist, which is why I didn't post my face."

"You could easily change your identity and out yourself."

Dixie knew Crystal was right, but she wasn't ready. Not while her breakup was still so fresh in her heart.

Crystal tilted her head. "And you don't make it easy for guys to want to become romantically involved with you."

If Dixie could count on anyone to be honest with her, it was Crystal. However, she hadn't anticipated Crystal diving in so deep, so fast. "What does that mean?" Dixie asked, though she pretty much already knew the answer.

"We've had this conversation a million times. You can come off as incredibly intimidating when people first meet you. But when you get to the one-on-one with a man, you put up a wall a mile high and make it impossible for them to climb it. And while I know you're comfortable with who you are, we both know you still have your mother's voice in the back of your head, and it comes out at the worst times, like first dates."

Dixie's biggest problem was that she allowed other people's perceptions—mostly her mother's—of her size to bother her to the point where she took those projections on as part of who she was, and that made it into her dating dialogue. She assumed that all men wanted a flat stomach, size C cup breasts, and not one single roll anywhere. "I know. You're right."

"So, what are you going to do about it?" Crystal asked. "And before you answer, no matter what you decide, I've got your back."

That meant the world to Dixie. She inhaled sharply and let it out slowly. If she was ever going to get out from under her mother's shadow, she had to move into the sunshine, as her father once told her. "If I'm going to keep *Create the Dew* alive, I need to start living what I'm blogging, and in order to do that, I need to put myself out there and get serious about dating again. But I don't want to get into a relationship necessarily right away. I need to be able to date so I can find the right person."

"I do know a guy I can fix you up with. He's sexy and a good person."

"That might be awkward," Dixie said.

Crystal nodded. "What about dating apps?"

"They suck." Dixie held up her phone. "I joined two this morning, and check out what I've gotten so far."

Crystal grabbed the phone. "Oh, God. These men are so not your type." She swiped her finger across the screen. "Boring." She jerked her head back. "Oh. This guy is so not right for you."

"I know. But what's a girl to do?"

Crystal set the phone down and took Dixie's hands. "I've got an idea. However, it requires you to be open-minded. Can you do that?"

"I can try." At this point, Dixie was willing to do anything. And not just for her blog. After reading the comments and putting herself out there to be criticized, she realized she was ready for a relationship.

She wanted what Crystal and her husband Albert had but didn't want to jump in with two feet. She wanted to test the waters. She wanted to be romanced. To have long walks. To go on picnics. To fall madly in love.

Dixie craved intimacy and romance. When

recovering from her anorexia and bulimia, she'd told herself that she'd stay away from men and relationships until she came to terms with how she'd ended up hating herself so much. She'd done that a while ago, and even though triggers—like her mother—brought back the kind of thinking that sabotaged Dixie's hard work, she always managed to get herself right back on track.

Except for when it came to men and dating.

In her day job as a relationship therapist, she dealt with couples struggling with things like sex, communication, and issues relating to betrayal. She didn't feel as though she needed to experience a long-term, committed partnership to help people navigate their predicaments because it came down to individual needs and desires being satisfied. Everyone dealt with interpersonal relationships differently.

But to write content on her blog about women taking charge of their sexuality, Dixie needed to at least have some clue about her own. And considering that she hadn't had sex in nearly eight months, her source material was sorely lacking.

"Have you ever heard of Club Allure?" Crystal asked.

Dixie's eyes grew wide. "I have."

"Well, Albert and I have a little experience with the club and some fetish festivals."

"Seriously?" Dixie lowered her chin and raised a brow. "I can't believe you've never told me about this. Do dish."

Crystal laughed. "I'm not going to get into the nitty-gritty, but I will get you in the club. I don't know if it's what you're looking for, but this might be able to help you with two things."

"What do you mean?"

"You can write about your experience in your blog. Just be careful what you put in black and white, and don't mention the club. That wouldn't be cool."

"Got it," Dixie said with her heart thumping in her throat. "Can't say I thought I'd be going to a sex club, though I've heard they have become very popular."

"Club Allure is a lot more than that, and it's not what you think. But it is going to change your world, trust me. You're going to do some soul-searching into your deepest, darkest sexual fantasies."

"Such as?" Dixie asked.

"Like do you prefer submission? Or do you

want to be a dominatrix? Are you into bondage? Are you—?"

"I get it," Dixie said, not wanting to dive too deep with Crystal, mostly because Dixie realized that her sex life could only be described as boring, like the flavor of ice. "Sort of. I mean, I don't know that I'm into *any* of that. I'm not really into kinky stuff."

Crystal laughed. "I've been reading your blog since you started it. You have your own set of fetishes. You just haven't acted on them. Most likely because you haven't found the right person—a *safe* person—to explore that side of you."

"Spoken like someone who has."

"You have no idea," Crystal said with a wicked grin and a wink. "But we're not talking about me. Check out the club. You don't have to partake in anything or hook up with anyone, but I think it might be just what you need."

"What's the second thing?"

Crystal picked up Dixie's phone and tapped at the screen. "The person I'm putting you in contact with at the club is the man I would have fixed you up on a date with."

"Oh. I wish you hadn't told me that." Dixie stared at the contact information Crystal had entered for a man named Zane. Her pulse picked up a notch.

"I won't tell him that I wanted to set the two of you up, but if you like him, feel free to make a move." Crystal leaned forward. "Or if you end up being too shy because of the club, call me later and I'll do it. But either way, enjoy the experience."

"I should be shocked you and Albert have been there, but I guess I'm not."

Crystal waggled her brows and gave Dixie a devilish smile. "Aren't you the one who said every couple has to find their sexual groove and that no man or woman should be shy about their wants, needs, and desires?"

"Unless they're criminal."

Crystal cocked her head. "Why must you do that?"

"Because I hate it when you toss my words back at me."

"Oh, Dixie." Crystal gave her a good squeeze. "It's time you got back in the game. I know Jeff did a number on you, but it's been like eight months since you dumped his sorry ass."

Dixie knew Crystal was right. Ever since she'd realized that Jeff would never leave his wife and that she was still allowing herself to be someone's second choice because she didn't believe she was good enough, smart enough, and sadly, pretty or sexy enough, she'd been slowly eating her way to ten more extra pounds.

Because that's what food did when she used it for anything but fuel. It didn't hear and support her. It only helped suppress and hide what was really going on. It was time she took her life back.

Again.

"So, who is this Zane guy, and how do you know him?" Dixie asked.

"He's a manager at the club and a good family friend. He's not a member or a dom or anything like that. He's just a guy. Give him a call and tell him I sent you. He'll show you around and answer any questions. He'll be your safety net. Remember, there will be lots of couples like Albert and me there. It's not some free-for-all sex orgy. A lot of committed partners who might be looking for a consensual threesome. Or those looking to bring someone into their marriage more permanently."

"I don't play well with others when it comes to my men—as we've learned."

Crystal laughed. "That is true. But something tells me that asshole ex-boyfriend of yours kept you to bland sex, and you're ready to spread your wings."

Dixie burst out laughing. "I can't believe you said that, and I'm so using that in my blog." She hugged her friend. "And for the record. Yes. Jeff was boring as fuck in bed. Despite my lack of trying to get him to step out of his comfort zone. Hell, his idea of being kinky was doing it with me bent over the dresser in the hotel room so he could look at us in the mirror."

"Doesn't every couple do that?"

"That's what I said. But he didn't even like it when I talked to him while we were having sex. Or, God forbid, asked him to try sexting." If Dixie were completely honest with herself, Jeff had been the kind of man she told women to stay away from. Not only because he was cheating on his wife, but also because he'd brought the ideals of being a man and the power that provided into the relationship. "He flipped when I randomly sent him a picture of the girls one day. He thought that was over the top."

"I'm glad you're not with him anymore and not just because of the vanilla sex, but he wanted a little woman to be at the door to greet him with a smile and a beverage. That is not you."

"You can say that again, sister." There was no

equality in whatever she'd had with Jeff, and even though she occasionally wanted to be dominated in bed, she didn't want that in her life.

Not even close.

"So, I'm just supposed to call this dude and say, 'Hey, show me around the sex club?'"

"Pretty much. Or if you don't want to hang around Allure, you could ask him on a date. Still, tell him I sent you. He'd actually know what that meant," Crystal said, glancing at her watch. "Shit, I didn't realize the time. I've got to get going. Let me know how it turns out."

"Wait. You told him you'd set him up?"

Crystal shrugged.

"Wonderful." Dixie sat on the bench, clutching her cell, watching the ferry dock at the port. Her heart hammered in her chest. If she didn't contact this Zane guy now, she'd keep putting it off until it was too late. She needed to get out of this funk before it became something deeper.

And darker.

She inhaled sharply, holding the cool Seattle salty air in her lungs for a count of ten before letting it out slowly.

She tapped the contact information and almost immediately got Zane's sexy, sultry voice message.

"Hey. It's Zane Pierce. I can't take your call right now, but leave a message, and I'll get back to you as soon as possible." He sounded like a cross between Keanu Reeves and Christian Slater.

Talk about dreamy.

His voice rolled over her senses like hot fudge melting on ice cream.

"Um. Hi. I got your number from my friend Crystal Morning about checking out Club Allure— not a date or anything." Shit. That was stupid. "Anyway, wanting to see if it's something I might be interested in. Crystal said I should call you to set up a time to check things out. You can reach me at 861-556-9326. Call or text, but texting will be best since I'll be with patients all day." With a trembling finger, she tapped the red button. "Holy shit. I can't believe I just did that."

Her phone vibrated in her hands.

She jumped, and the cell flipped out of her hands like a fish out of water, flopping on land. A rollerblader had to make a quick move not to run it over—or her fingers—as she reached for it. "Sorry," she mumbled.

Thankfully, the screen hadn't cracked since she'd neglected to put her case on… per usual.

Zane: *Hi, Dixie. This is Zane. Got your message.*

Crazy morning. Let me know if you're free tonight. I can put you on the list as my guest—not a date, haha. How does 8 sound? Just text to confirm and I'll send the information on how to get in and all the protocols.

"No way." All the air in Dixie's lungs flew out like a bird diving into the water on a mission to find its favorite meal. She hadn't expected him to get back to her in a matter of minutes.

Or to get an invite to an exclusive sex club so quickly.

But she'd be damned if she backed out now.

Dixie: *That's perfect. Thank you.*

If nothing else, she would give the readers of *Create the Dew* something to get a little hot and bothered over.

Part of Zane's job at Club Allure with new membership was to ensure that the privacy of those in attendance was respected. However, he hated doing deep-dives on people's social media accounts. This one should be easy. She came recommended by a club member.

The wife of a cop.

A close personal friend.

He blinked. Crystal had always been kind to him and it shouldn't surprise him that she wanted to fix him up. The fact that Dixie had made mention of it made him wonder if she'd turned down the date in lieu of getting into Allure. It shouldn't bother him, but in a way it did. Crystal wouldn't consider him if she didn't think Dixie was his type.

He rubbed his eyes and stared at the computer. There was nothing worse than trying to do due diligence with a potential client who barely existed on social media.

Dixie Gaynor barely made a dent on the internet. About all she had was a professional photo plastered on a website regarding her business. Turned out Dixie was a relationship expert. That explained the comment in her voicemail about seeing patients.

Zane couldn't help but wonder what kind of kink Dixie was looking to satisfy. He'd seen it all during his years at the club, and he'd learned that most realized sex and love always went hand in hand. He just wondered when *his* ship would arrive.

Staring at Dixie's photograph, his blood pumped a little faster. Her lips were plump and kissable. He could tell she had something special that made her stand out in a crowd. If he saw her in a bar, he'd definitely introduce himself, but she'd opted for the experience of Club Allure and not a date. He had to respect that.

He dropped her face into an image search, but

since it was black-and-white, he found nothing. Of course, Dixie could be a nickname. She could have a different name elsewhere on the internet. Wouldn't be the first time, except that had been her name on her professional LinkedIn account, so that blew that theory.

He scratched the side of his head. Very few ladies under the age of thirty-five didn't have an Instagram account. Then again, Dixie dealt with couples and their struggles both in and out of the bedroom. He suspected that she needed to keep a safe distance, and being easily accessible through social media might be a recipe for disaster.

Zane's job was to protect the club and everyone involved. Therefore, he needed to find out as much as he could about Dixie. Crystal had referred her, and Crystal's husband happened to be a cop.

That should be enough.

"Yo, Zane. " Some chick named Dixie is here for you," Erik, one of the security guards, said. "She said Crystal sent her?"

"She's right on time," Zane said. "What's she like?"

Erik leaned against the doorjamb and fiddled with his wedding ring. They'd come to an understanding, but working together still had its awkward moments. This could prove to be one of them. "She's a knockout for one. And as usual with anyone new, she seems a little nervous." Erik handed Zane the interview forms. "Why do you ask?"

Zane ignored the question. For now. "Did she say anything revealing? Anything that might help me guide her to what she really wants?" People who came to Club Allure either knew exactly what they were looking for or had no idea.

She obviously fell into the latter, but sometimes, those who worked the club could easily sense a new client's tastes by their initial reactions.

Erik shook his head. "I trust my instincts, and I think she's a tough one to crack. I doubt she even understands why she's here." He narrowed his stare. "You haven't answered my question."

"Which one?"

"Don't act like you and I don't know each other," Erik said. "You always want to know about what our impressions are. What we think the customer is looking for. Not a routine *what are they like*."

Zane let out a long breath. He'd made a

promise to Erik that his friendship was important. When he'd made that statement, he'd meant it. Still did. Erik never held back when Zane asked, so why should this be any different? "Crystal first offered to set her up on a date with me, but she opted for a tour of the club instead."

"I see." Erik arched a brow. "Are you interested?"

"I have no idea. Until a few minutes ago, I didn't even know what she looked like. It was just weird. That's all," Zane said. It felt good to open up to Erik. They needed this conversation. "Send her back. Oh, and welcome home. I hope you and Lenny had an awesome honeymoon. I mean that."

"I know you do." Erik smiled. "Your support has always meant the world to us. Things only got weird because of Rebecca." He turned on his heel and headed down the hallway.

Zane smoothed down the front of his slacks and did a quick check in the mirror, tucking one side of his long, wavy hair behind an ear. Not that it mattered, but he always liked to dress to kill. And even though he'd only seen one black-and-white picture of Dixie, he more than liked what he saw. She had soulful eyes and they spoke to him in a way that no other woman had in a long time.

He glanced down the hall, and the air in his lungs escaped. He tried to take in a deep breath but couldn't. He gasped. His heart dropped to his gut like a ton of bricks as the most beautiful woman he'd ever seen strolled down the plum-colored carpet with her head held high. Her long, brilliant copper-red hair bounced over her shoulders with just the right amount of curl to drive a man wild. His fingers itched to take that crimson hair and tug.

Her hips swayed back and forth like one of those momentum ball things his grandfather used to have on his desk. Like the rest of her body, her hips were round and voluptuous—like a lady's form was supposed to be—with curves in all the right places.

And her plump, rosy lips?

They didn't disappoint.

Christ. All he could think about was how they'd feel pressed against his as he took them in a hot, powerful kiss.

Sweet temptation.

That's what Dixie Gaynor was. And it would take all his resolve not to talk her out of finding whatever it was she was looking for at the club and talk her right into his bed.

"You must be Dixie," he said, stretching out his

arm. His blood raced through his body in anticipation of feeling her skin against his.

"I take it you're Zane." She blinked once as her long lashes fluttered over her bright teal-colored eyes that reminded him of the Caribbean Sea at sunset.

Tiny electric pulses tickled his fingertips and worked their way to his brain, sending him into momentary shock. He held her fingers for what he knew to be longer than appropriate.

Screw it.

He lifted her hand and kissed the back. "Welcome to Club Allure."

"Thank you."

"What do you think so far?"

"I've only been in the main bar and lounge." She raised her index finger to her mouth and nibbled on her nail. "I didn't expect it to be so… large."

"Would you like a tour of the place?"

God, how he loved the way her porcelain cheeks blushed with a hint of red, and how her green eyes widened with a combination of excitement, fear, and curiosity. Only it was driven because of the club.

Not him.

Something that drove him crazy with jealousy, and that wasn't an emotion he was used to.

"Can I ask a crazy question?" she asked.

"Of course. That's what I'm here for."

"What exactly am I going to see while on this tour?"

"Why don't we start with a drink in the main bar, and we can go from there?" He placed his hand on the small of her back, resisting the urge to run his fingers up to her bare skin.

She wore a yellow dress with straps that fell off her shoulders. The material hugged her full-figured body in all the right places, and he couldn't rip his gaze from her if he tried.

"The one with the stage?" she asked quietly.

"Yes. It gives you an idea of different options you can explore." How he wished she'd prefer to explore him instead.

"How long have you worked here?"

"Going on five years." He slipped into a booth in the main room. A few doms entertained a couple of new young ladies while a dominatrix and her sub were having a drink with a couple who liked to have their fantasies played out in front of them.

"How did you hear about the club?"

"My brother lives the lifestyle of a dom and brought me on." A few more members strolled in, and the excitement in the room built. Couples kissed and touched each other intimately as they waited for the fuel that would turn their fire into an inferno.

"Is your brother here?"

"His wife is pregnant. Due in two months. They haven't been around in a while." Zane almost never discussed other members, but his brother always allowed it. And he could talk about Crystal, since she referred Dixie.

"Did they meet here?"

"No. A mutual friend of theirs introduced them." Zane tapped his finger on the table and pointed toward a couple. "Those two are into being in the dominant role together, so they often find a submissive here for play. Is that something you'd be interested in? I could introduce you." He nearly choked on the words.

Thankfully, Dixie shook her head quickly.

He hoped that whatever this sexy young woman was into, he might be able to fulfill the desire. Only he couldn't do it on company time.

Not if he wanted to keep his job.

Nor could he make the suggestion.

"Do you like red wine?" he asked.

She nodded, glancing around the room. Her gaze landed on the center stage where demonstrations took place.

He glanced at his watch. One would begin in about ten minutes. He motioned to the bartender to bring over two glasses of his favorite blend. He looped his arm over the back of Dixie's seat, letting his fingers toy with the soft strands of her hair. His job was to make new potential clients feel comfortable, but this went too far and could be seen as grounds for dismissal.

He'd never wanted a woman as much as he wanted Dixie. And something told him that his desire would go beyond the physical hold she had on his mind, body, and soul. "Much of what goes on here in the main room is geared toward the dominant and submissive. Whether it be a man in the dom role or a woman, that is up to the individual and the couple, though we have a lot more men doms, as you will see."

"Do you have anyone who swings both ways?"

Zane laughed. "It doesn't work that way in the club. You'll see submissives kneeling for all doms. It's a sign of respect. They call them 'Master.' So, inside Club Allure, once a submissive, always a submissive. But what people do behind closed doors outside of here, as long as it's consensual and not illegal, that's not for us to judge. You have to remember, this is a sexual appetite. A desire. It fills a void, fulfills a need."

"What about you? What are you into?" she asked.

"We're not here for me, now are we?" He handed her a glass of wine the waiter had brought over and tapped his against it. "Tonight is about you and finding out if the club has something to offer you and your needs." He pointed toward the center of the room. "Sit back and relax."

"What's happening?"

"A demonstration of what happens between a dom and his submissive. How safe bondage is. How it doesn't hurt. It shows how the submissive has power and control while letting the dom have his way with her, all while maintaining mutual trust and respect." Zane inched closer, feeling the heat from her skin clinging to his body. He'd sat with other women during demonstrations before. While watching was always a turn-on, it was never something that excited him in a way that he wanted to experience it sexually.

Much less wanting to share the experience intimately with the woman sitting next to him. This was new territory, and he had no idea what he was doing.

"We're going to sit here and watch?" she asked.

He nodded. "It's all part of Club Allure. And it might give you a better understanding of your true desires and fetishes, and how best to fulfill them while in a safe environment."

Her beautiful cheeks turned even redder.

He loved her innocence. Because, deep down, he knew there was nothing sexually innocent about Dixie. Being submissive might not be her thing, but when she found what she wanted, he knew there would be no stopping her.

He just hoped he would be able to find a way to be on the receiving end.

Fuck. How did one woman get under his skin in a matter of thirty minutes?

He didn't get out enough.

She leaned forward, resting her elbows on the table as she stared intently at the couple. The dom ordered his submissive to kneel and put her hands behind her back, and she did just that.

Dixie flinched when the dom used a flogger on his submissive.

Zane refrained from putting his hands on Dixie, even though he wanted to reassure her that the lady was enjoying every second with her master. The experience was as sexually satisfying for her as it was for the dom. Maybe even more. The trust one had to allow someone to take charge was unique and when a sub found their dom, it was magical.

Not that Zane had ever tried either role. He preferred a more yin and yang kind of experience. But he wouldn't mind being tied up a time or two either with the right partner.

However, instead of watching the demonstration, like Zane often did during these tours, he kept his focus on the beauty sitting next to him, enjoying her reactions.

Her tongue took a long, slow, broad stroke over her pink lips before she took a sip of her wine. Her chest rose and fell slowly, and under the fabric of her dress, he saw her nipples tighten and pucker.

He rubbed his thumb and forefinger together.

As things heated up onstage and got rougher, Zane shifted uncomfortably in his seat. He'd seen almost everything in the club, and not once had he ended up with a full-on erection.

His desire had nothing to do with the dom and

his submissive and everything to do with the sexy woman sitting next to him.

Dixie glanced in his direction.

He swallowed.

Hard.

"Would you like to do that to a woman?" Dixie asked.

He tore his gaze from her to the stage and back again. "No. I'm not into whips and things like that, though I would never deny a woman—that I was in a relationship with—her desires, so I could be open to it." Shit. He shouldn't be talking about himself. "Would you like to be on the receiving end? Because you can give it a try, tonight if you'd like. That master is open to more than one submissive. He's not exclusive, and demonstrations are also about experimenting."

"God, no. If I'm going to do anything like that, it's going to be with someone I know and trust."

Zane leaned close, his lips only an inch from her ear. "Sometimes a stranger, or someone you just met, is the best person to try something new with." Quickly, he leaned back and pointed at the couple. "Keep watching." He downed half his beverage.

Talk about torture. He didn't think he'd make it

through to the end of the night without making a total fool of himself.

She bit down on her lower lip, and he imagined her doing that very thing in the throes of passion—with him.

He couldn't stand it anymore. He had to touch her, if only to feel her skin on his fingertips. He rested his hand on her shoulder and gave a little squeeze. "Are you okay?"

She nodded; her breath came in short pants. If he wasn't mistaken, she moaned.

"You like this. You like watching them, don't you?" He ran his fingertip across the side of her face, tucking her hair behind her ear.

"I've fantasied about watching people have sex, but I've never done it before like this," she said with a breathy, raspy voice. "With an audience."

"Just pretend the rest of us aren't here. That's what everyone else does." He massaged her neck, hoping to ease the tension that had slipped into her muscles. And his.

She leaned a little closer, dropping her hand to his thigh.

He groaned.

He was crossing every line.

He should move a few inches away, putting

space between them. He'd be fired if any of the higher-ups were anywhere near this room tonight.

Letting his fingers glide down her back to the side of her dress, he found the swell of her full breast. He studied her expression as she arched her back, shifting her body and giving him better access.

He traced a path on her skin as she heaved in oxygen. His finger got caught in her cleavage. He wiggled farther inside her dress until he found the object of his desire.

Her eyelids fluttered shut as he flicked his finger over her hard nipple.

He glanced around the room. No one was looking in his direction. They were either having their own fun or immersed in the demonstration, as they should be. That's what Club Allure was all about.

Satisfaction.

Desire.

Passion.

The sweet temptation he felt to lower her dress and take her nipple into his mouth nearly overtook him.

Until her hand slid up his thigh and squeezed.

He groaned as he leaned back in the booth. He

gripped her breast a little harder than he probably should have, but she didn't seem to mind.

Her deft fingers worked the button at the top of his slacks, and before he had a chance to even blink, she had his shaft in her hand, her thumb running across his sensitive tip.

He tried to find his voice, but even if he did, he wasn't about to ask her to stop—though that's exactly what he needed to do. What his job required him to do.

His lungs burned with every breath he took. His toes curled as he tried to maintain control, but Dixie didn't care. She gripped harder and stroked faster. He placed his hand on her hip, sliding his fingers over her round ass. He gritted his teeth. He shouldn't be letting her take him like this, in a booth at Club Allure.

But he wasn't about to stop. He loved every second. It was the most erotic thing he'd ever experienced.

"Dixie," he whispered. "I can't hold off any longer."

"Good," she said, not turning her head, her gaze still intent on the couple on stage, now demonstrating the finer points of bondage. She cupped him, squeezing even harder.

"Jesus," he said under his breath. He reached under the table and curled his fingers over her hand, guiding her, if only to put himself out of this torturous, glorious misery. His climax came hard and fast, and he did his best to keep his guttural groan as quiet as possible.

He inhaled sharply, trying to regain his composure.

Dixie slipped her hand from his and raised her fingers to her lips. Her tongue darted out of her mouth and licked.

"Good Lord, woman. You're going to be the death of me."

She jerked her head and stared at him with a slackened jaw. Her green eyes grew wide with the kind of shock that came with fear.

And maybe regret.

Fuck.

"I've got to go," she said as she stumbled from the table. "Sorry."

"Wait." He went to stand up and then remembered that wouldn't be a good idea. "Dixie. Don't leave like this." He fumbled with his pants as the beautiful redhead in the yellow dress raced out of the room. "Dixie," he called as he jumped up from the table and made a beeline for the entrance.

But by the time he got to the parking lot, all he saw was brake lights.

Shit.

Not only would his boss have his head, but Crystal would probably give him an earful.

Worse, he'd just freaked out the woman of his dreams.

4

Zane opened the door and frowned. "Not that I don't love spending time with Reid, but I thought you were coming alone." He stepped to the side and let his cousin and her husband through the door.

"You said you needed relationship advice and he's the expert on that. Not me."

"That's not what I said." Zane shook his head as he made his way back to his kitchen and opened the fridge, pulling out a couple of beers. He handed one to Reid before offering Darcie water.

"Doesn't matter. He's better at matters of the heart." Darcie climbed up on the stool at the island in the center of his kitchen. "Besides, it's date night, and before we know it, we're going to be tied to a baby. When we're done here, we're going out to eat."

"You could have declined," Zane said.

"That's what I told her." Reid held up his beverage and clanked it against Zane's. "But she was insistent. Something about wanting to know what you fucked up so royally."

Zane wished Crystal had been available, but she had plans. He'd texted with her a little bit about the situation, leaving out most of the details and all she had to say about it was: *Ask her out. Just do it. Don't stress over whatever happened at the club. I'm sure the two of you can have a nice dinner and work it out.*

If Crystal only knew the dirty details.

Zane leaned against the counter by the sink. He needed advice and Darcie and Reid could provide some, even with limited knowledge. "What I'm about to share, you have to promise will stay between the three of us."

"I won't breathe a word to anyone," Darcie said.

"We don't know each other that well, but you can trust me." Reid nodded.

Zane chugged his beer. He couldn't mention Crystal because he had no idea if Reid knew she and her husband were members. Most likely, he did, but just in case, it was best if Zane kept names out of it. "So a friend offered to set me up on a date, only the girl in question decided on taking a tour of Club Allure instead of going out with me."

"Maybe the girl in question wanted to know if you were into all the sex stuff at the club over being into a monogamous relationship." Reid arched a brow.

That was a good point and one that Zane had considered over and over again. But if that were the case, he didn't want to be involved with her. He'd had enough of women who were into games. He wasn't a member of the club. He worked there. He didn't play there.

Until the other day.

"I can't be involved with any members or potential members. So, this lady is hands off, only her hands were all over me and I didn't stop her," Zane admitted, holding up a hand to keep Darcie from interrupting him. "It's not what happened that I'm concerned about at this juncture, but the fact she's not responding to my texts or calls. She ran out of the club right after and hasn't spoken to me since."

"Wow. That's brutal," Reid said.

"She could simply be embarrassed," Darcie said. "I've never been to the club and have no intention of ever going, but I have a few friends who are members, and I know it can be hard-core."

"Sweetheart, you're making this adventure enthusiast want to try it more." Reid laughed, holding up his hands. "I'm joking."

"You better be." Darcie nailed him dead center in the chest with her index finger.

"I am, but my darling wife has a good point. This girl is probably embarrassed, especially if she initiated the sexual contact, in your club, knowing she could have been on a date with you. That makes it so very personal."

"I know. That's why I should have stopped her," Zane said. "But I was so attracted to her."

"Was this *she's hot; I want to get laid* attraction?" Darcie asked. "Or the kind of desirability that gets under your skin, that you can't shake and that keeps you thinking about a person at night."

"The latter," Zane said. "While I enjoyed what happened, I don't care about it. What I want is to get to know her, but she won't respond, and now I'm coming off as desperate and pathetic. I honestly don't know what to do."

"Is she the kind of woman who might be into flowers?" Reid asked.

"I have no idea. I asked a mutual friend about

that and chocolates. I'm waiting to hear back since I don't want to make it worse for myself," Zane said.

"That's smart." Darcie sipped her water. "But I'd also stop texting and calling. At least for a day or two. Give her time and space to consider her feelings about what happened. And you have to be prepared to let this go."

Zane lowered his head and his gaze. "I don't know if I can do that."

"Why not?" Darcie asked.

"I know this won't make any sense, but I care about her like I haven't cared for anyone in years."

"Then don't make the mistake we made," Reid said. "Hound her until she hears you."

5

Dixie sat on her back patio overlooking Lake Washington outside of Seattle with a tall glass of white wine and a low-calorie snack. She'd been really good with food all week, and she wouldn't ruin it now. Still, she wasn't about to give up alcohol.

Not tonight.

She'd spent the last five days avoiding the texts on her phone and the three voice messages from Zane.

She knew she needed to respond. His messages were sweet and kind, and he seemed concerned about her feelings.

She topped off her wine and took a few more

sips before lifting her cell and finding the string of texts from Zane.

Zane: *I got your number from your interview paperwork. Call me. Please.*

Zane: *Why did you run out? We should talk. Please call me.*

Zane: *I don't like how we left things. Please. I just want to talk.*

Zane: *Dixie. I just want to talk. That's all.*

Zane: *Call me. Please. I'm begging. I can't stand how you ran out.*

Zane: *I just called and left you a long-winded message. I feel really bad about you leaving the way you did. Call me. Or text. Just let me know if you're okay.*

She didn't bother reading the rest of the messages since they were more of the same, nor did she relisten to the voicemails Zane had left. She owed him an explanation and it would be better in person.

Dixie: *Sorry I've been ignoring you. I have no excuse. You didn't deserve that. Are you available tonight to meet and talk?*

Bubbles appeared immediately.

Zane: *Yes. I'm not working this evening. Where would you like to meet and when? I'm free now and for the rest of the night. Name the place and time and I will be there.*

Wow. She wasn't sure if that seemed desperate…

Or insanely sweet.

She glanced at her glass of wine and realized that it wouldn't be smart to drive, and she had no desire to get in a Lyft.

Shit. She hadn't thought this through well enough.

Dixie: *Come to my place. Give me forty-five minutes to deal with some things, and if you don't mind, bring some dinner. I've got white wine open. So anything that goes with that. I'm easy.*

Shit. Too late. She'd already hit send.

Zane: *Do you have a grill? I've got steaks that I was going to cook. Doesn't go with white, but I've got a bottle of red I'll bring. You good with that?*

Dixie: *Sounds perfect. See you soon.*

She sent one last text with her address.

Now, she had to write a blog post.

She needed to come clean with her readers about a lot of things. In an authentic way that wouldn't come off as if she were seeking sympathy or looking for attention.

Those two things were not her intention. Her blog was meant to help people. To give them something to relate to and help empower them to take charge of their lives and their sexuality.

She wanted her readers to own their bodies. Their souls. Their personalities.

Not to feel shame for being true to themselves, no matter their life choices.

While her blog was more geared toward women, it was meant for everyone and anyone who needed and wanted support. She wholeheartedly believed that men could get just as much from reading her blog as females could. Yet, even with that, it didn't matter to her if a woman wanted to be a stay-at-home mom or a career woman who never had the desire to get married or have children. She wanted to empower women to embrace the choices men took for granted. She admitted to herself and the world that her voice and words were meant to touch a woman's soul. To guide them on their journey. But when a man stumbled on her site, she hoped he could at the very least relate in terms of the women in his life.

She flipped open her laptop and poised her fingers over the keyboard.

First, I want to apologize for being so quiet this week. I had an experience that required much reflection—both in regard to my current life and my past. For the last six months,

I have been writing to you nearly two to three times a week about how to take charge of your life, both sexually and otherwise.

And yet, I haven't been able to do that with mine.

You see, I've been hiding behind my anonymity.

And my pain.

And not just with being a plus-sized woman—because I truly do love my body. When I look in the mirror, I see a sexy redhead with a lot of fire and passion. However, I allowed the world to steal my thunder. I let the voices from my childhood tear me down. I let the looks and stares from others when I was on the beach in a two-piece make me want to cover up.

Not for me.

But because my extra rolls make them uncomfortable.

No matter how many times I hit the reset button, it's hard to always see the beautiful woman I am, both inside and out. I can't let a negative comment or two on my blog—or elsewhere for that matter—meant to 'motivate' me to lose weight be the defining moment in my life anymore. I did that before, and I almost died to achieve and maintain that. It can't define me any longer.

And neither should it with any of you.

Sure. I know there's a fine line between being in denial about one's weight and being active, healthy, and eating right.

I just choose not to deny myself life's simple pleasures.

I like my wine.

Cheers.

I like my cake.

And I eat it, too.

Everything in moderation.

So, I say, have a small slice on your birthday. Or at a wedding. No need to have it every day. Don't binge. Don't make excuses. Eat the broccoli too. The point is that we make choices, but we have to make sure they are truly the right ones.

I'm proud of who I am, and yet, part of me is ashamed. Why? Because of some life choices that made me feel like a fraud. And if I'm going to help you navigate the path to loving yourself, your relationships, and your sexuality, then I have to be open and honest with you.

So, I'm going to start with my identity.

I'm not Dew. My name is Dixie Gaynor, and I'm a relationship therapist. I have a private practice and have been working in this capacity for three years. I have a doctorate in psychology and decided to specialize in relationships because I come from a broken home.

She reached over her computer and snagged her wine, downing half of it. Her mentor would have a field day with her revelation.

If she only knew half of what Dixie was about to admit.

Oddly enough, I became involved with a married man.

Yes. I know. That is a terrible thing to do. In my defense, I didn't know he was married. But when I found out, I didn't end the relationship. I fell for the old 'I'm going to leave my wife for you' line.

Something to this day I wish I hadn't done.

But I can't go back and change it. I can only learn from it and use how it's affected me going forward. And truth be told, I've allowed it to keep me from being… me. I used it to keep myself in a cycle of self-pity and self-hatred.

This brings me to sex and sexuality.

Before I allowed myself to be in a relationship that all but stole my voice as a woman, I had been searching for the kind of man who would build me up. One who would respect me and want to share my hopes and dreams.

And my sexual desires.

Last week, I had a sexual experience that was not only totally unexpected, but also something that I would never do yet had fantasized about before. The problem is, I took off after, and haven't spoken with the man since.

Something I need to rectify.

I got in over my head, and while I don't regret what happened, I do regret running out. Sex, even if it's a one-night stand or with a stranger, is nothing to be ashamed of, as long as it's consensual and what you both want.

No matter what you are into, even if it's being submissive, or a dom/domme, or watching others have sex, or just plain bland style, if it's what you and your partner enjoy, then it's the most beautiful and perfect thing in the world.

The key is to be comfortable with yourself.

And your partner.

You need to share with your lover what you desire. If you can't do that, then do you want to be in that relationship?

On that note, this blog is taking a slight shift. I will still continue with tips regarding relationships and sexuality, but I will be sharing with you my own personal journey as well.

If I ever have one.

Being single and plus-sized is difficult.

Men don't see me the same way they see a girl who is a size six. I hate to say that, but it's true.

Granted, the gentleman I had this wicked experience with a few days ago didn't seem to mind my body, but I must come clean.

He didn't see me naked.

He got a hand job.

That was all.

It was a really wicked one that left us both breathless, and the circumstances were hot and sexy and like nothing I've ever experienced before. It scared me in part because I felt connected to him in such an intimate way, yet I'd just met him.

I hope he felt the same way about me, but I don't know. And I won't know unless I do something about it.

That's the hard part about all of this.

I'm going to put myself out there and see if he's interested in something more. If not, well, you'll be the first to know. If he is, again, you'll be the first to know.

Stay dewy.

Dixie.

She uploaded a picture of herself in the yellow dress she'd worn the night she went to Club Allure.

Without filters.

Before she could think twice, she hit publish.

It was a good post. Real. Honest.

She leaned back, raised her glass, and smiled. "Bring on the trolls." She laughed. Of course, there would be negative comments. She'd always gotten them. Her philosophy had been that she didn't exist if she didn't have haters. But she worried maybe she'd gone too far.

"Hey, Siri. Call Crystal Morning."

The cell rang twice.

"Hey, girl, what's up?"

"I posted on the blog," Dixie said. "I want you to read it."

"Okay. Hang on."

A long silence filled the night air. Dixie closed her laptop and leaned back on her chaise lounge, gazing at the millions of stars filling the cloudless sky.

A rare evening in Seattle.

"Holy shit," Crystal exclaimed. "You little dominatrix. Why didn't you call me?"

"Because I needed some time to sort through my feelings. I'm not a dominatrix, and I sure as shit don't want a submissive man in bed. At least not all the time."

"Only *some* of the time?" Crystal asked with amusement. "So, who was the hand job man?"

"I'm not telling you that," Dixie said. "And I'd appreciate it if you didn't go poking—"

"I can't believe you'd even think I would," Crystal said. "I'm just glad you enjoyed yourself."

Dixie let out a short laugh.

"You *did* enjoy yourself, didn't you?"

"Yes, I did. But there are consequences."

"Do you like this man?" Crystal asked. "Was it Zane? Because if it was—"

"For the record, I don't know the man." Not a total lie.

"Well, if it makes you feel any better, I didn't know Albert the first time. But I trusted my instincts, and look at us now."

"That does help." Dixie let out a long breath.

No way in hell did she regret what she'd done with Zane. She'd been taken by surprise, but never in her life had she felt so in control and powerful. She knew without a doubt that he'd loved every second, too. He would have done anything she'd asked in that moment.

Within reason.

But the best part was that he'd wanted exactly what she'd given him. He'd craved it. Desired it. Right then, in that space and time, it was the perfect sexual encounter for both of them.

Mutually gratifying.

She needed nothing in return, only it would have been nice if she'd had the wherewithal to stick around and finish her drink and maybe have a normal conversation to complete the fantasy.

"Then what's the problem?" Crystal asked.

"Me. I've been lying to my readers. More importantly, I've been lying to myself." She glanced at the time. Thirty minutes before Zane showed up. "I've been afraid to really put myself out there and live my life. It was easy to stick with Jeff, a married man, who would never truly be with me. Love me for me. It was safe. This? Taking a risk with this guy I just met? Scary as hell. I mean, he's like no man I've ever dated. Besides being a nice guy, his body is like a Greek god's. But I still have that little voice in the back of my head that says: *You're too fat. He's not going to like to see you out of your clothes.*"

"That's your mother's voice."

"Doesn't matter. It's there. But I'm going to get rid of it once and for all." And Zane would help her do it. "I've got to get going, Crystal. I have a date."

"You go, girl. Let me know how it works out."

"Will do." Now, all she had to do was figure out what to wear so she didn't look like she planned to seduce the man.

But that she'd be open to the idea.

6

Zane bent over and tugged at the ponytail holder, letting his long hair bounce to his shoulders. He ran his fingers through the wavy locks. He'd always thought his hair was one of his better assets.

Satisfied that he looked halfway decent, he snagged the bag of groceries from the back of his Harley and made his way down the walkway, impressed by her stylish abode. She obviously did well for herself in her career.

Nothing was sexier than a successful woman who took charge of her life.

A slight breeze kicked in, bringing with it the salty scent of Seattle. A layer of mist filled the air as low-hanging clouds descended from the sky. Most people hated living in Seattle because of the dark, chilly days, but this ambiance made Zane's heart beat a little faster. He raised his hand and rapped his knuckles three times against the blue door with its small hanging basket of flowers, the blooms greeting her guests with an array of spring scents that tickled his nose and brought a smile to his soul.

That seemed so like something Dixie would do.

He inhaled sharply, preparing himself for the onslaught of sexual tension that had already begun to build, starting in his toes and slowly crawling up his skin, leaving a scorching trail of tingling heat in its wake.

The door swung open, and there stood Dixie in a pair of jeans and a strapless floral top that flowed down to the middle of her thighs.

He swallowed, trying to keep the air in his lungs.

Once again, she stole his breath.

"You look stunning," he managed.

"Thank you."

He reached out and lifted a strand of her wavy hair from her shoulder. "I love this color."

"It's not natural."

He smiled. "I don't care. It's beautiful on you." He leaned in and kissed her cheek, letting his lips linger as he inhaled the scent of her sweet strawberry shampoo. He cupped the back of her neck before running his hand over her shoulder and down her arm. "Though now I'm curious, what is your natural color?"

"I'm a redhead, just more of a light red, not this bright copper." She glanced up at him and blinked. She couldn't be taller than five five, giving him a good nine inches on her, though when he'd seen her last, she'd been wearing heels.

Tonight, she was barefoot.

He liked that.

Taking her chin between his thumb and forefinger, he pressed his mouth to hers, slipping his tongue between her plump, rosy lips. He pulled her tight to his chest, deepening the kiss. He wanted to take her right here in the hallway. Slam her against the wall and rip her pants to her ankles, ramming himself deep inside, making her gasp for air.

He broke off the kiss and took a step back. Before he took things to the next level, he needed to find out why she'd run off the other night. He needed to understand what had prompted her to be so intimate at the club and why she ignored him after. His heart couldn't afford to be broken again. He held up the bag. "Where's the grill? I've got some prime steaks to cook up for us." He smiled. "And some wine that needs opening."

She took the bottle. "Follow me."

"Hmmmmm. Gladly." He tucked one side of his hair behind his ear and stared shamelessly at her round ass as she led him through the family room, the kitchen, and finally out onto the back patio that overlooked Lake Washington.

However, the only thing he saw was Dixie.

He hadn't noticed anything else.

She turned and leaned against the railing. The sun tried to peek through the haze, but it was halfway behind the mountains anyway. Soon, it would be dark, and the pitch-black sky would cast the eerie canopy Seattle was notorious for, blocking the stars and making it impossible for the moonlight to punch through the clouds.

But the sound of the water gently lapping at the shore and the soft lighting from inside was all they needed to create a sexy and romantic atmosphere, making it nearly impossible for him to remember all the questions that loomed in the back of his brain.

He set the bag of groceries down on the side of the grill and caught her gaze. "I'm glad you finally called." He fired up the cooking apparatus and began preparing both the meat and the veggies he'd brought. It took his mind off the sexy woman and kept it on why he wanted to chat.

"I'm sorry it took me so long. I could say I was busy with work, but that would only be an excuse."

"It's okay. I just wish you hadn't run out the way you did. Especially after what happened."

"Me, too," she said.

"Can I ask why? Did I do something wrong? Because I thought it was amazing and wicked, though I wouldn't want you to think that I introduce every woman to the club like that. Actually, if anyone found out, I would be fired on the spot."

"Well, I won't tell anyone." She took a corkscrew and worked on the wine bottle, twisting and turning. It only served as a reminder of the other night.

"It's important to me that you know I've never been with a woman who's been to the club." Zane closed the lid to the grill and took the glass she offered. He studied her as he took a few slow sips of the full-bodied cabernet. It was one of his favorite blends, yet it was under thirty dollars a bottle.

"I hope you don't find me rude, but that's hard to believe, considering how easily it happened."

"Only because I find you completely irresistible." He lowered his chin and arched a brow. "I'm finding it difficult to stay over here by the grill and cook the food when what I *really* want to do is get you out of those jeans and return the favor."

She waggled her finger. "Using the word *favor* just pushed you back into the friend zone."

He tapped his chest. "Ouch. Why?"

"Giving you an orgasm shouldn't be considered a favor just because I didn't have one. Would you expect me to *return the favor*?"

"Ah, I see. We're going to play the semantics game." He tossed his head back and laughed. "If I'd said I wanted to make you come like you've never come before, would that be acceptable?"

She held her wineglass near her full breasts and nodded as she swallowed. "Sex shouldn't be tit for tat."

"No. But I wouldn't want you feeling anything but fully satisfied. Did you feel that way when you ran out of Club Allure?"

She shook her head. "But not because I wanted more than what happened. I didn't. Honestly, that was the fantasy."

"You've daydreamed about watching bondage and jerking someone off?"

She nodded. "Not necessarily bondage or in a club. But watching someone have sex while giving a man a hand job, yes. Only my fantasy ended with dinner." She laughed. "I mean. Finger-licking, normal conversation, and bread-breaking. Unfortunately, I freaked out."

"Why?"

"I felt like I took advantage of you. And then I just didn't know what to say. I don't normally behave like that."

"Trust me. I would have stopped you if I didn't want you to do that." He quickly lifted the grill cover and poked at the steaks, flipping them and adding the foil package of asparagus. "I think it was exactly like you to do what you did. You've just never taken control of your sexuality."

She raised her glass. "You have no idea how funny that is."

"Enlighten me."

"I'm a relationship counselor, and one of the things I specialize in is helping couples take control of their sex lives."

"Always easier to talk about it than to implement it in your own life." He didn't like how she danced around the core issue and avoided what really bothered her. Until she was willing to put it out there, it would always be something between her and any man she got involved with—only he planned to do his best to make sure he was her last stop. "So, you're really not embarrassed or ashamed by what happened between us?"

Her pretty little cheeks flushed red. "I wish I could say I wasn't at all, but part of me is a little."

He closed the gap between them and wrapped his arms around her, heaving her against his chest. He cupped her face, brushing his thumb across her cheek. "It was one of the most incredible experiences I've ever had. You left me breathless and speechless." He took her hand, placing her index finger on his lower lip before sucking it into his mouth. He let out a guttural moan. "When you licked your fingers with me still on them, I lost all ability to think straight. And then you were gone."

"I'm sorry. I realized that night that all the issues I thought I'd conquered, I really hadn't. And they all hit me at once."

"That makes me sad. But whatever or whoever those issues are, I'm not them." The sound of meat sizzling reminded him that he was supposed to be cooking dinner. "Why don't we spend tonight getting to know each other better?"

"Sounds perfect. I'll go get some plates." She

scurried off to the kitchen. He let out a long breath. Whoever hurt her or gave her the wrong idea about herself would have to deal with him. Because no woman as sweet and special as Dixie should be made to feel as if she didn't deserve the world on a silver platter.

7

Thus far, they'd kept the dinner conversation light. They'd discussed movies and books and other first-date material topics. Things they both wanted to know about each other, but not the one thing she knew he was most curious about.

And, of course, Dixie had her own list of interesting questions she wanted Zane to answer and it was time to shake things up.

"Why work at Club Allure if you're not into bondage, being a dom, and all that?" Dixie asked.

"I was interested in trying it, and my older brother is a master, so he introduced me. I sat and watched a demonstration and knew instantly that the lifestyle wasn't for me. At least not like that, with all the strict rules. I wouldn't want any woman kneeling or calling me sir or master. Nor do I want to do that in reverse—though I'm more apt to give a woman whatever she wants in the bedroom when she demands it. I like to please. That satisfies me the most."

"Anything?"

"Within reason. I do have a few hard nos."

"Such as?" She pushed her food around on her plate.

"I'm not interested in threesomes. I've tried them and it's not my thing," he said, raising his glass. "I don't like to share."

"I'm the same way, though I've never tried one, and I can't say it's something I'm interested in. Too many hands and pieces to figure out what goes where."

He laughed. "It does get interesting."

"And you've never hooked up with anyone at the club?"

He smiled that wicked, sultry grin of his that made his eyes twinkle like shooting stars. "I've been with someone who works at the club, but never the patrons. Until you."

"I won't be a patron. Club Allure isn't for me."

"My boss will be sorry to hear that. And even

though my job is to sign you up, for selfish reasons, I'm glad you don't want to be a more permanent member. Though I could tell you enjoyed watching."

Her insides heated as if she were lying in the hot sun. Her nipples puckered. She took a small bite of her steak and chewed as delicately as she could. She still hated eating in front of men, but she'd made a decision to change, and that started now.

"I did. But I could watch porn with my partner," she said.

"It wouldn't be the same. It would be like doing a virtual hot air balloon ride and making the assumption that you've experienced not only the view but also the exhilaration of being a few thousand feet above the Earth." He winked.

"Not a good analogy. I can't say I've ever had the pleasure of being in a hot air balloon."

"Oh. You have no idea what you're missing," he said. "But as far as watching, there are other places and festivals that would give you—*us*—the same opportunity. Or other options if we wanted. And I'm not saying I'd want it all the time, but I wouldn't be opposed to doing that again."

"For a guy who says he's not into the scene, you

sure are interested in all the things Club Allure has to offer."

He raised his glass. "No. I'm just into you."

"Oh. Flattery isn't necessarily the way you'll get me naked." She tapped her glass against his and took a hearty sip. "Tell me about your last girlfriend."

"Last girl I dated, or last serious relationship?"

"Both," she said.

"Well, last girl I dated ended recently because she didn't like me working at Club Allure, which I can understand. I'm not opposed to finding a new career, I'm just not into ultimatums, which she gave me."

"Oh. That's not cool," Dixie said. "Okay, what about the serious relationship?"

"Not much to tell. We were together for a year. She was the jealous type. Again, that doesn't go well when your boyfriend works in a sex club."

"Is that why you broke up?"

"That was only one part of it," Zane said. "I'm a private person, and she betrayed my trust."

Dixie narrowed her stare. "So, you broke up with her."

"It was just best for us to end it."

"Where is she now?"

"Dating some dude from her work. I think she's happy, which is all that matters."

"Did you love her?" Dixie really wanted to know what this chick looked like and if she was a size two or not, but she had no idea how to ask that without looking like an asshole.

"I cared about her, but I wasn't in love with her. So, in the end, it was for the best. Now, what about you? What was your last relationship like?"

"Not great, to be honest."

Dixie didn't want to have the conversation about her ex-boyfriend who'd been married, because it always ended with a discussion about her blubber—and ultimately, her mother. But given how Zane stared at her with his piercing dark eyes and bombarded her with probing questions, she knew he wouldn't let up.

"How so?" he asked.

"We just weren't meant for each other."

"Come on, Dixie. Why won't you answer my question? I answered yours."

She stared down at her plate, which was now devoid of the asparagus and about a third of her steak—the rest she'd cut up and pushed around her plate.

Sadly, she was still hungry.

Zane had managed to scarf down all of his and now picked at the cheese and crackers she'd put out.

She'd noticed him glance with an arched brow between her lips and her plate.

"There is never a good way to bring this up, and I'm probably jumping to conclusions, but I can't help it based on the way you're dodging my question and avoiding the food on your plate." He set his glass down a bit harder than usual, and some of the red liquid sloshed over the sides. "Is part of the reason you weren't meant for each other because he's an asshole who took issue with your beauty?"

She pressed her hands against the table, ready to lay into him about how everything wasn't always about weight. Only she didn't expect him to deflect the obvious and flip it to make it sound as if Jeff were just a moron who didn't know a good thing when he saw it.

"That's an interesting way of asking whether Jeff didn't like my figure." She forced herself to take another bite, resenting the mental sound of her mother's voice, telling her she should have gone for a dry salad or perhaps only a glass of water.

As if that would fill her up and nourish her body.

"If he had a problem with your size, he's a dick."

"He's an asshole for more than that reason," she said, letting out a long breath. She stabbed two pieces of meat and placed them on her tongue. She had to admit, it was the best steak she'd had in a long time. She shoved her plate to the side since she was finally full. She wiped her lips with her napkin.

"What was the sex like with your ex?" Zane asked.

She coughed. "I'm glad you waited until I was done eating to hit me with that not so great segue." She took her wine and moved from the small table down to the lower part of the deck, closer to the water.

Zane followed.

"I told myself for a long time that I was comfortable with my body. And for the most part, that's true. I love myself for who I am. But being with Jeff was one of those life decisions that kept me from actually accepting it." She turned, catching Zane's sweet, empathetic gaze. It was hard to concentrate on anything but him when he stared at her that way.

"My mother is perfect. Physically. Of course, she's had countless procedures to stay that way. But her looks are her business. She's a walking advertisement for her practice and weirdly proud of that fact. She's still a size four and doesn't have a wrinkle or an age spot on her body. To her, the only way to keep a man satisfied is if you dress up his arm."

"First, I don't know what dressing up someone's arm means, but wouldn't that be up to the man to figure out what he likes and finds desirable?"

She opened her mouth, but Zane held up his hand.

"And that goes for a lady, too." He ran his hand through his wavy hair. It bounced to his shoulders. "I'm sure there are women who find my hair unruly and would prefer someone with a clean-cut look." He lifted his shirt, showing off a tattoo of a sailboat on his chest.

His nipple was right smack-dab in the center of the wheel.

"And I've got eight more tatts on my body. Maybe people find that unattractive. I don't want to be with a woman who wants to change me or judges me for my decisions—both good and bad."

She raised her finger to her lips. All she could think about was sucking on that nipple. She shook her head. "You're pretty hot."

"Thanks. So are you. And it bothers me anyone

would make you feel less than beautiful. Especially your own mother."

"It's hard for me to believe that sometimes." She inched closer and covered his mouth with her hand. "And that has nothing to do with me not loving my body, and everything to do with the way the world views overweight women." She dropped her arm to her side. "People say things like, '*Oh, you have such a pretty face,*' as they look me up and down. And both my mother and Jeff… would say things like, '*Are you sure you want to have a bagel? Carbs are your enemy.*'"

"Unless you ask for someone's help with your food intake, they shouldn't say anything."

"Well, Jeff thought he was doing me a favor," she said. "The worst was when he told me how his wife lost the freshman fifteen."

Zane took the glass from her hand and set it on the end table by the outdoor chaise lounge. "I'm glad you're not with him anymore. He doesn't deserve a woman like you."

"What does that mean?" She held her breath as Zane brushed her hair back from her face and wrapped his strong arms around her body.

His hands made their way down her back, lifting her shirt and finding her bare skin.

"Confident. Smart. Sexy. Kind. Did I say sexy?"

She smiled. "You did." *Don't ask the question. Don't do it. You don't want to hear the cheesy, ridiculous answer that is only a half-truth.* "What about me is sexy?"

"When I opened my office door last week and laid eyes on you, I knew I was a goner." He brushed his soft, hot lips over her cheek. Then the other one. His hands curled over her ass, pulling her even closer.

"Why?"

"You strolled down the corridor with a massive amount of self-assuredness, a tinge of sweet innocence, and a dollop of sexiness that made me want to get to know you better—if you had any interest in me."

She stared deep into his dark-chocolate eyes as she ran her fingers through his soft, thick hair. "I have to know something."

"What?"

"Everyone has a type."

He arched a brow as his hands glided up her back and unhooked her bra. "You're my type." He leaned in, but she tilted her head back.

"Some men like large breasts. Others prefer big butts."

"Are you going to tell me size matters? Should I be worried?"

She laughed. "I've seen and felt the goods. You've got nothing to worry about. And now you're the one deflecting."

He narrowed his eyes, and his expression turned serious. "I like my women smart and to know what they want. And I like curves. I don't like girls who are so skinny I'm afraid I'll break them." His eyelids fluttered, and he groaned. "You're the sexiest woman I've ever met. Both inside and out. And I can't wait to find out what will make you call out my name as your body quivers under my touch." He lifted her shirt.

"What? Here?"

He nodded.

She glanced around. It was one thing to give him a hand job in a club where half the room was fucking. But in her backyard? Where any boaters driving by could see them?

Though it *was* getting dark.

But the lights would still illuminate her deck.

She held up her bra as he tossed her shirt to the side.

"You're cute when you're vulnerable," he said. "If you're really that uncomfortable, we can go inside. Whatever will make you the most at ease. But I want you right here, right now." He traced a path down her jaw, across her neck, and to the center of her cleavage. "Was the other night the first time you've ever done anything like that in public?"

"Yes," she managed, dropping her hands to her sides. Her bra fell to her feet.

He took a step back and licked his lips. His hands cupped the underswells of her breasts, and his thumbs gently rolled over her hard, tight, tingling nipples.

The world around her blurred. She couldn't catch her breath. He'd barely touched her, yet every inch of her body lit up as if she were on fire.

"I know this is a weird question, and not that I ever want another man in our bed, but you never really answered my question about what the sex was like. And I'm asking about with anyone."

"It was okay."

He kissed her neck just under her ear. "Sounds like it's been boring."

"Pretty much."

Swiftly, he turned her, pressing her against the railing. He cupped her breasts and wedged his knee between her legs.

She blinked and stared at the lights dancing on the lake.

His hands massaged her body while his lips did the tango across her skin.

"I don't want you to ever settle for *okay* again. Tell me what you like. What you desire. What you need." He pinched and twisted her nipples and sucked on her earlobe.

She opened her mouth, but no words formed. She tried again. "This works."

He chuckled, and his hot breath left her gasping for air.

Her lungs burned. She gripped the railing and focused on the gentle waves lapping against the breakwall.

Carefully, he undid her jeans and lowered them to her ankles, then helped her step from them. He ran his hands up and down her legs while dotting hot kisses to the backs of her knees. Her inner thighs. He tucked his fingers into her boy shorts, tugging at them, then rolling them over her hips. She'd never been with anyone who understood her body the way Zane did.

He gave her the kind of attention she'd been craving her entire life.

"Turn around, please," he whispered.

She resisted the urge to cover herself as she rotated.

"You're so fucking gorgeous." He pulled his shirt over his head and just stared.

She took a strand of her hair and twisted it between her fingers.

"That's hot," he murmured as he inched closer. He lowered his head and took her nipple into his mouth.

"Oh, God." She clutched at his head, threading her fingers through his long, wavy hair as she watched.

He glanced up and smiled before nibbling on her tight bud with his teeth.

She bit down on her lip and held him steady. "Don't stop."

"How about if I add this?" He glided his fingers up her thigh, finding her hard nub. He wiggled gently and then dove deep inside before repeating the action.

Her breathing became labored. She couldn't form words if she tried. She shifted her body, lifting her leg.

Before she knew what was happening, he pulled her into his arms and carried her to one of the chairs. "This might be a more comfortable position for you where you can also watch." He sucked on two of his fingers before driving them into her shamelessly.

She gripped his shoulders and gasped.

He repeated the motion. "Do you like this?"

"Yes." She slid her hand down her stomach and joined his hand, much like he'd done with her the other night.

"That's it. Show me."

Never in her life had she touched herself in front of a man, but Zane watched intently as she pleasured herself.

Then he batted her hand away. "My turn."

He repeated exactly what she'd done. Only better.

And then he spread her legs wider and lowered his head.

She gathered his hair in her hands and sat up a little taller. She needed to see him giving her the pure passion she'd denied herself, even during the years she'd believed she was this great sexual being who loved her body.

She'd accepted that she was a plus-sized girl.

She'd accepted she was a loveable woman.

She'd even accepted she was a sexual being.

But she'd never believed that she deserved the

kind of satisfaction she told her patients—or those who read her blog—they should demand from their partners.

The slow build began at her toes and inched up past her calves.

He caught her gaze and held it for a long moment while his tongue did what could only be described as the most wonderful dirty dance imaginable. He brought her to the edge but didn't let her go over.

Then he did it again.

And again.

Until she couldn't take it anymore. Only she wanted her release to happen when he was inside her, not like this. Not this time.

"Kiss me," she demanded.

"I am."

She tugged at his hair, pulling his mouth to her lips while frantically unbuttoning his pants and yanking at them. She shoved him into one of the chairs and pulled his slacks and boxers to his ankles before tossing them to the side. In all her sexual experiences, she usually avoided being on top. Or in a seated position. And now that she was climbing on top of him, she understood the real reasons why.

No matter who she'd been with, there had been

a small bit of shame about her size. It wasn't because she didn't love herself or her body, but rather because the men she'd chosen to be with, while they cared about her, still wanted her to be different.

Smaller.

Worse.

Sexier.

But not Zane.

He grabbed her hips and thrust up into her. Hard.

She arched her back and groaned, holding his shoulders, digging her fingers into his skin.

He hissed. "I have no control with you." He cupped her breast, drawing her nipple into his mouth, laving it with his tongue.

Her climax grew deep in her gut. Her muscles trembled. "Zane," she whispered. "Yes." She dropped her forehead to his and stared into his dark eyes. Their bodies moved as one. "Zane. Now. I need it now."

He slipped his hand between their bodies, finding her swollen nub. He flicked it gently but firmly, sending her into a tailspin. As she convulsed, shaking uncontrollably, he gripped her hips tight, thrust deep inside, and spilled his climax with the same passion and fire as he had the other night.

While she exploded into a second orgasm. "Oh, my God. Zane. Yes."

Cupping her face, he kissed her lips with sweet tenderness. He filled her with a combination of passion, desire, and temptation. Wrapping his arms around her, he nuzzled his face against her neck. "Best dessert I've ever had."

She giggled like a silly schoolgirl as she relaxed against his strong body. Normally, she'd be looking for a blanket to cover herself.

But not this time.

Not with Zane.

She rested her head on his shoulder and kissed his neck. "Thank you."

"For what?"

"I don't know. Dinner and a couple of orgasms?"

He brushed her hair from her face. "You're welcome." He kissed her nose. "You should know I'm a one-woman kind of man, and I want you to be my one special lady. Are you up for that?"

"Hell, yes."

He laughed. "You're not going to get jealous of me at Club Allure?" He took her chin between his thumb and forefinger, tilting her head. "I love my job. I'm not giving it up."

"I wouldn't ask you to." She ran her hand through his gorgeous hair. It wasn't right that he had better hair than she did. "I might have some body-image issues, but I'm not a jealous or insecure woman. Still, I do have a question about that."

"Okay."

"Am I allowed to come to the club?"

He laughed. "I can make some arrangements during my days off for us to go if that's what you want."

"I might like that." She sat up, cupping his face. "Want to go skinny-dipping?"

"I thought you'd never ask."

8

"**W**here are you taking me?" Dixie glanced out the window of her car. Zane had to practically pry the keys from her hands. It wasn't that she didn't like people driving her vehicle. But she preferred to be in control, and she didn't like surprises. "Why are we getting off here?" Butterflies filled her stomach as they headed miles south of Seattle, closer to the Sound. In the distance, she could see Vashon Island.

Zane stretched out his arm and squeezed her thigh. "Relax."

"Easy for you to say. You know the agenda."

"You say that as if I have something nefarious planned."

"For all I know, you do," she said with a playful

tone. Over the last couple of weeks, she'd gone from single and ready to mingle to happily attached without so much as a wandering eye.

Well, maybe she had glanced a time or two. Who didn't? But no one compared to Zane.

No one.

He laughed, a deep, sultry sound that ignited her insides. "You're going to love this."

"Like I loved '*Let's recreate the scene from the movie* 9 ½ Weeks *where we feed each other random things blind-folded…* and you fed me cauliflower mash, and I almost barfed on you?" While everything else about that night had been sexy as hell, she could have done without that part.

"Lesson learned. You don't like cauliflower no matter how doctored up it is with sour cream, bacon, and chives," he said. "Any food involved in today's festivities will be of your choosing."

A thick lump formed in her throat as they pulled into the parking lot of Up in the Air, a local hot air balloon adventure tour. "You're joking, right?"

"No. You mentioned you've never been, so I thought it would be fun."

"Is your superpower remembering everything I say?" She held on to the clasp of her seat belt as if it were a lifesaving apparatus, and she'd fallen into the ocean. She blinked. Thankfully, she hadn't said that out loud, or next thing she knew, she might be scuba diving.

Something that wasn't on her bucket list.

He leaned in and kissed her cheek, his hot breath sending warm chills across her skin. "No. My superpower is giving you regular—and multiple —orgasms."

"I doubt that will happen at five thousand feet while I'm utterly terrified. I'm afraid of heights."

"That family over there will probably be in the balloon with us anyway, requiring us to keep it PG-rated." He took her chin between his thumb and forefinger. "Are you the kind of afraid everyone is while on a plane, but you get on anyway? Or is it the paralyzing kind? Because if it's the latter, I'm the world's worst boyfriend. For the second time."

She palmed his cheek and stared into his dark gaze that always gave her strength and comfort. "I'm right in between the two. And you're the best boyfriend ever." She brushed her lips over his, promising what might happen later—when they were alone. Perhaps even on the car ride home. "I've always been too timid to do something like this. I would never go on my own, and if you'd asked, I would have said no."

"If you want to back—"

She covered his mouth. "Don't give me the option. I need to step out of my comfort zone. I mean, people go up in those contraptions every day, and nothing happens to them. Right?"

"Right." He tapped her nose. "Besides, I'll be holding on to you the whole time."

"Awesome. We can plummet to our death together." She unhooked her seat belt.

He groaned. "Now you're giving me second thoughts about my decision to sweep you off your feet—quite literally." He stepped from the car and jogged around the hood.

She'd never tire of watching how his hair got caught in the wind or how he smelled a little bit like morning dew on a chilly fall day. When she'd stepped into Club Allure, she'd been looking to jump-start her dating life.

Not find a man who made her heart swell with something akin to…

No. She wasn't falling in love with him.

Heavy *like*? Absolutely.

And it helped that he was damn fucking good in bed.

He laced his fingers through hers and tugged her in the direction of the big, floating balloons.

A man wearing a pair of low-hanging jeans, boots, and a cowboy hat strolled by—more like sauntered. He had that blond-haired, blue-eyed movie-star quality that was hard to miss.

"So, you like cowboys, do ya?" Zane said, giving her a little hip check.

"Not sure I'd kick him out of bed."

"Neither would I," Zane mused.

She glanced up at him, and he winked. But something told her he wasn't kidding, making her want to give him an extra treat on the ride home. She had no clue why she was so turned on by the idea that he might have been with a man once in his life or that he'd perhaps fantasized about it. But she was, so she rolled with it.

Zane checked them in while she stood and stared at the balloon. Her heart beat so fast, she thought she might spontaneously take flight.

They'd lucked out with the weather—which was nothing short of a miracle in Seattle. A few big, puffy white clouds floated overhead, but the sun had command of the sky for the most part. She pulled her sweater across her body as a breeze came in off the Sound.

She hated flying, but she loved the last twenty minutes, where she got to see all the details of the world below.

"How are you holding up?" Zane asked as he looped a protective arm across her shoulders.

Craning her neck to catch his gaze, she smiled. "I haven't vomited out of fear, so that's good."

"We're both going to love it. I just know it."

"You've never done this?"

He shook his head. "But I have gone skydiving, so if I can jump from a perfectly good airplane, I think I can handle this."

"You're not hiding a parachute or any other surprises anywhere, are you?"

"Nope." He kissed her temple. "I've got you, babe."

Two teenage boys raced by, shoving each other and laughing. They stopped near who Dixie assumed were their parents and stood in front of the steps to get into the big basket hanging by mere ropes and tied to fabric that could easily tear.

She blew out a puff of air. Thankfully, she hadn't said that out loud. If she weren't careful, her sarcasm would ruin the day, and that was the last thing she wanted. Zane had gone out of his way to do something special for her.

Jeff had never done that.

Not even her mother had taken the time to make Dixie feel as though her thoughts and feelings were the most important things. Not even on her birthday. Hell, she'd once video-called the day after Dixie's birthday, arguing that she knew damn well what day her daughter had been born. Dixie had to pull out her driver's license and prove to her mother she'd missed it by twenty-four hours.

Nothing about today was special.

Except for the fact that she'd be spending it in public with the man who'd managed to make her not think about how his waistline was smaller than hers.

The pilot—or the aeronaut, as he called himself—went over the safety measures and procedures for their flight.

Dixie hung on his every word, memorizing the details, while the two teenage boys seemed more interested in their social media accounts.

"Ready?" Zane asked.

"Born ready," she said, taking his hand. She climbed into the basket and flung herself at Zane.

"Whoa." He fell back against the side of what could only be described as a wicker laundry basket attached to a partially inflated oversized kids' balloon.

The boys laughed.

"I think maybe I want to just stand in the middle," she said, hugging Zane tightly.

"I suggest you hang on to the side. Standing in the center, you'll get bounced around. Trust me," the aeronaut said.

"Come on." Zane helped her ease into one of the corners. "Grab hold of the side. I've got you. Promise."

She nodded, ignoring the peanut gallery commenting on her fear while the boys' parents quietly scolded them and then politely apologized. Instead, Dixie focused on the feel of Zane's arms around her body, making her feel cared for and protected.

As the helium filled the fabric, the basket shook.

Zane kissed her temple. "I've got you, babe."

"What are we, Sunny and Cher?"

"God, I love your humor." He brushed her hair from her face and quickly tied it back in a low ponytail at the nape of her neck.

She sucked in a deep breath as the balloon slowly took flight. Her stomach floated to her throat, dropped back down, then rose again.

It did that about four or five times as they lifted higher and higher.

She dared to take a peek over the side and gasped. "It's so beautiful up here," she said quietly. The boats in the Sound became smaller. In the distance, she could see more of the islands and the ferries bringing both tourists and locals from one glorious stop to the next.

No view was like this one.

She turned and blinked out a tear. "Thank you."

He brushed her cheek. "I seem to have made you cry. That is never my goal."

She smiled. "These are happy tears. And this is the most beautiful gift anyone could have ever given me."

"You won't be thanking him when we land," one of the boys said. "It's not always fun."

"So not cool, dude." Zane arched his brow.

"Hey, young man. Apologize right now," the mom said as she tugged at the boy's ear.

"It's okay," Dixie replied. "Thanks to this guy. A bad landing is not only worth the view, but it's worth the risk." She palmed Zane's cheek and gave him a more PG-13-rated kiss—tongue and all.

9

Zane sat outside of Dixie's office building and tapped the photo icon on his cell. He couldn't go an hour without looking at a picture of her. How had he gotten so lucky as to land such a sweet and sexy girl?

It had been nearly two months since they'd started dating, and he knew she was the one.

The only one.

He'd fallen head over heels in love with Dixie Gaynor.

Zane: *Hey, babe. How's your day going? Almost done?*

He glanced at the time. He was fifteen minutes early, and it was possible she was with a patient. When the bubbles appeared immediately, it shocked him but excited him more.

Dixie: *Just finishing up paperwork. Did you hear from your brother?*

Zane: *Still at the hospital. Still no baby. He said it could be a while.*

Dixie: *Are you sure you want to go to this party? You don't have to come with me if you'd rather go be with your family.*

Zane: *I want to come. I want to meet your friends now that we are all official. Besides, there is nothing I can do at the hospital but sit in a waiting room. As soon as Gayle has the baby, I'll go visit them.*

Dixie: *Okay. But you can back out at any time. However, I have to warn you that my cousin is like a big brother to me, and he can be overprotective. He's been weird about me 'hiding' you all this time. His wife isn't any better. So, be prepared for some obnoxious questions.*

Zane: *I'm sure I can handle the big-brother type. I'm in the parking lot. Ready whenever you are.*

Dixie: *On my way down.*

Zane leaned against his pickup. He preferred his Harley, but it was supposed to rain. Besides, Dixie wasn't a huge fan of his motorcycle, and he was all about pleasing his girlfriend.

Girlfriend.

Wow.

He didn't think he'd be thinking in those terms

after his last one plastered their failed relationship all over *Page Six*. Of course, that's what he got for dating an actress, but still. His sexual tastes didn't need to be exposed to the world. Not that he cared if anyone knew he'd once dabbled in bisexuality. That was his business, not anyone else's.

In actuality, his only grievance with Rebecca had been that she'd made public their private life, and only because she wanted to hurt him. In the process, she did a world of damage to other innocent people who had nothing to do with their problematic romantic entanglement.

The building's front door swung open, and the most amazing woman in the world stepped into the sunlight. Her bright-copper hair bounced over her shoulders, and she smiled.

"Hey, good-looking," he said as he pulled open the passenger-side door. "Your chariot awaits."

"Mmmmmm. Aren't you sweet?" She patted his chest.

He pulled her close, pressing his mouth to hers, slipping his tongue between her lips. Shamelessly, he squeezed her ass. God, he loved everything about this woman. He never wanted to go a day of his life without her in it. "This might not be the best place to do this, or the most romantic, but I need to tell you something."

"Oh. That sounds slightly ominous."

"Not really," he said, tucking a piece of her thick hair behind her ear. "I want you to know that not a minute goes by that I don't think about you."

"Just so you know, I have it on good authority that you are most likely going to get laid tonight."

He chuckled. "Good to know, but not where I was going with this."

"Okay. Then I'm all ears."

It shouldn't be so hard to get out three little words, but he found himself sweating and speechless.

"Dixie, you rock my world."

"That's it?"

He shook his head. "This isn't going as planned." He rested his hands on her hips and stared into her sweet green eyes. "You are the sun to my sky. The moon to my night."

"I've never seen you this corny."

"Oh, wait. I'm sure I'll come up with more weird, subpar, not-very-romantic crap," he said with a nervous laugh. In his thirty-one years on this planet, he'd loved only once, but that relationship had been vastly different. Looking back, no one had ever stolen his heart the way Dixie had. "But in the meantime, you should know that I love you," he said. The last time he'd said those words to a woman, he hadn't meant them. And it had cost him dearly.

But Dixie would never betray his trust, this he knew deep to his core.

Her green eyes grew as wide as the Emerald City. "You what me?"

"You heard me."

She stuck her finger in her ear and wiggled it. "They must be full of wax because I could have sworn you said you loved me."

"I did." He swallowed his beating heart. "Too soon?"

She shook her head. "No. I'm just… just… stunned."

Shit. His mother had always told him that wearing his emotions on his sleeves was both a blessing and a curse. "You don't feel the same—"

She covered his mouth with her hand.

"Oh. No. I love you, too. I just don't know that I'm ready for this."

"You and me both," he said. "There is something else I need to tell you." He knew he should have told her about his past sooner. Probably before he declared his love, but every time he thought it might be the right time to bring it up, he either chickened out or something came up.

She tilted her head. "You're not a natural brunette?"

He would never tire of her quick-witted remarks. But when she got scared or concerned, she sometimes used them to deflect. "There's something from my past that I kind of left out."

"As long as you're not secretly married or have a bunch of kids somewhere, I don't care."

He laughed. "It's nothing like that."

"Well, there are a few things I haven't told you about me, too."

He arched a brow. "A few?"

"Okay. Just one."

"Looks like we both have confessions to make." He held her tight, not willing to let her go. He loved everything about her, so whatever this little revelation was that she needed to get off her chest, he figured it would be no big deal. He just hoped she was open-minded about the fact that he had once been in love.

And it had been with a man.

His phone buzzed in his back pocket. He held up his hand. "Let me check in case it's Xavier."

"I totally understand." She tossed her purse in the passenger side of his truck.

"It's my mom." He glanced at Dixie, tucking his hair behind his ears. "Hey, Mom. What's going on?"

"Oh. Zane. It's not good."

"Mama. What happened?"

"We don't exactly know. Gayle was having a difficult delivery, and they decided to do a C-section. Something happened. They took the baby to the NICU, and Gayle is in surgery. Your brother is beside himself. They won't let him see his child, and we have no idea how Gayle is doing."

"I'm ten minutes from the hospital, Mom. I'll be right there." He shook out his trembling hands. "I have to go. My brother needs me."

Dixie circled her arms around his waist and kissed his neck. "Of course. And you need me."

"No. You go and be with your friends."

"I'm not leaving your side." She took his hand. "You're trembling." Reaching into his pocket, she snagged his keys. "I know what your family means to you, especially your brother. Now get in the pickup. I'm driving."

"What would I do without you?" He pulled her

in for a warm hug, pressing his lips to her forehead. "But no one but me drives Bessy."

She tipped her head back and blinked. "Bessy? You couldn't come up with a better name?"

"My last truck was Stella."

"Now that's sexy." Dixie jogged around the hood of his truck.

He stood there with his hands on his hips and shook his head. "Um. Didn't you hear what I said?"

"I did. But I'm not just anybody. I'm the woman you love. Besides, I let you drive Jack."

"Who the fuck is Jack?"

"My car." She slipped behind the steering wheel and patted the cushion on the passenger seat. "Get your ass up here. Your family is waiting for you."

"I love it when you boss me around."

"Don't I know it."

He buckled himself in and stretched out his arm, taking her hand. "My mother has been dying to meet you."

She groaned. "I didn't think this through."

Zane laughed. "Too late now." He tightened his grip. "I hope everyone is okay by the time we get there. Xavier might be a dom at the club, but his wife wears the pants at home. They've been wanting a family for a while now."

"Try not to let your mind start going down the worst-case road," Dixie said as she maneuvered his truck into traffic with ease.

Impressive.

But, of course, she was *his* girl so he shouldn't be surprised. Dixie could do anything she put her mind to.

"Easier said than done. My mom doesn't panic easily, and she sounded scared."

"Hospitals can be scary places in general," Dixie said. "My mom works there. Let me give her a call and see if she can get us some information. Okay?"

"That would be great, but I know you don't talk much, and I don't—"

"This is different. I'll call her as soon as we get there."

"I love you, Dixie. I really do."

10

"There's my little pumpkin," Dixie's mother said as she stretched out her arms.

"Hello, Mother." Dixie's skin prickled. She glanced over her shoulder, thankful that Zane was nowhere to be found.

"I hate it when you call me that." Her mother leaned in and gave her a quick air peck, completely missing her cheek.

Well, Dixie couldn't stand being reminded that her mother looked at her as if she were the actual size of a rounded jack-o'-lantern, but she wouldn't call her out on that.

For now.

"Sorry. I'm just worried about Zane's family."

"Where is this Zane fella?"

"I think he went with his father to go find some real coffee," Dixie said. "Have you been able to find out anything about Gayle?"

"Not much, except that she's still in the operating room," her mother said. "I just got out of surgery myself. But what I do know is that she's in the best hands possible."

"Can you give me something for her husband? All he knows is that she started hemorrhaging, and then her blood pressure bottomed out. Next thing he knew, he was being kicked out of the room, and his baby was being whisked—"

"The baby is stable. You know that." Her mother took her by the shoulders. "I'm going to see if I can scrub in. But it's only been a little over an hour. I'm sure Gayle will be fine."

"Thanks, Mom. I appreciate it."

"Excuse me," Zane's aunt said, holding out a tray of fresh, home-baked treats and sandwiches. "Dixie. You must be starving. I know we pulled you and Zane from a dinner party."

"Thanks." Dixie's stomach growled. Loudly. She sucked in a deep breath and reached for one of the egg salad rolls.

"Dixie. You don't want that." Her mother actually slapped her hand. "I've got a salad in my office. I'll bring that down for you a bit later." Her mother smiled. "Let me go see what I can find out." And with that, her skinny-assed mother disappeared.

Dixie took two sandwiches and a cookie. "Thank you. I really appreciate it."

"There's more where that came from." Zane's aunt squeezed her shoulder. "We're very grateful you're here."

Dixie needed a few minutes to clear her head.

And stuff her face.

She took a stroll through the halls of the pediatric wing, nibbling on one of the sandwiches, eating slowly until she was full. No point in going back to her old habits. She wrapped the other one and placed it in her purse. She'd be hungry later. For now, she enjoyed the cookie and made her way back to the waiting area. She scratched and rubbed the side of her neck. She always felt like she was breaking out in the worst case of hives every time she came within a hundred feet of her mother.

"Are you okay, dear?" Zane's mother, Anita, asked as she looped her loving arm around Dixie's waist. "You seem upset."

"Hospitals have that effect on me."

"I consider myself a good judge of character,

and I'd say it's not the surroundings. It's more one particular person who seems to get under your skin." Anita arched her brow just like her son would. "Come, sit with me." She nudged Dixie toward a table in the waiting area outside of the nursery where they'd transferred baby girl Pierce, and Xavier currently spent his time.

"Your granddaughter is beautiful." Dixie stole a glance into the nursery before sitting down with Anita.

"Yes. She is. I'm just a little surprised she's so bald. My boys were born with about as much hair as they have now."

Dixie laughed. "It's sad when you're jealous of your boyfriend's hair."

"I wish the circumstances under which we met for the first time were a little less stressful." Anita patted her hand. "I haven't seen Zane so happy in a long time, and I have a feeling it's because of you."

"I don't know about that."

"A mother knows these things. A mother can tell when her son is head over heels in love. And Zane loves you. Do you love my son?"

Nothing like being put on the spot. But there was no point in lying. "Yes. I do."

"Good. That's good." Anita's smile faded. "I'm

sorry you have some struggles with your mother. I never had a daughter; I understand those relationships can be difficult. Whatever the issues, don't forget you're making an effort. You're the one putting yourself out there. But the only person you ever have to please is yourself." She pointed toward Zane and his father, strolling down the corridor in their direction. "Even the men we love don't get to tell us how to feel or who and what we should be. A good man will stand by and support you and help you through anything. And so would a good mother. I know. I shouldn't judge. And this isn't my place. But I heard what she said to you when my sister brought over all those snacks."

"Oh. I see." A twinge of shame tickled Dixie's heart. But she wasn't sure if it was because she was embarrassed by her mother's behavior.

Or because she was still struggling to accept that some people honestly didn't see her as a heavy person.

Only as a person.

"I don't know your mother. And I'd like to believe that all parents do things because they think it's what's best for their children." Anita shook her head. "I've certainly said some stupid things to my boys over the years." A single tear rolled down her cheek. "When Zane struggled with his sexuality and dated a man—"

"He dated a man?"

Anita gasped, covering her mouth. "Oh, no. Me and my big mouth. Is that going to be a problem for you?"

"No. I don't judge. I work with a lot of bisexual couples. It's all part of my job. He just didn't tell me."

"Zane is such a private man. Getting him to tell us anything about you was like pulling teeth at first. But you're all he talks about in the last couple of weeks. It's Dixie this and Dixie that. So, I figured he might have told you about that time in his life."

"We're still getting to know each other. And he did mention before we got the call about Gayle that he needed to tell me something about his past."

Anita closed her eyes. "He will never forgive me for telling you."

"He'll never know you brought it up."

"Thank you." Anita squeezed Dixie's hands before she stood and made her way across the room to her husband.

Dixie pushed back her chair. Suddenly, strong arms surrounded her body and she felt a kiss on her neck. "You and my mom are hitting it off," Zane said.

"She's a lovely person."

"The best."

Dixie turned, rested her head on his shoulder, and squeezed her eyes tight.

"Hey. What's wrong?"

"Nothing."

"I call bullshit." He took her chin between his thumb and forefinger and tilted her head. "Your eyes are wet with tears."

"It's been an emotional hour."

"You let your mother get to you. She said something, didn't she?"

"She means well." Dixie rose on tiptoe and pressed her lips against his in a tender kiss. He'd become her entire world, and in only two short months. "I love you," she whispered.

"I love you, too."

His brother stepped into the waiting room, raking his hand through his hair. He plopped himself down on one of the chairs. "I can't do this," he said. "I can't keep holding her and telling her that it's going to be okay when I don't even know what's going on with my wife." He ran his hands over his face. "Have we heard anything?"

"My mother was going to try and scrub in," Dixie said. "That was about fifteen minutes ago."

"Thanks." Xavier nodded. "I appreciate it."

Anita sat down on one side of Xavier while Candor, Zane's father, made himself comfortable on the other side, looping his arm around his eldest son's shoulders.

Dixie's mother burst into the center of the waiting room with dramatic flair, pulling off her mask. "I have good news."

Xavier was on his feet in seconds. "Good news? My wife is okay?"

"Yes. They are moving her to recovery. You'll be able to see her in half an hour or less."

"Oh, thank God." Xavier broke down. Tears poured from the man's eyes. He hugged his father as if he couldn't hold his weight.

"Mom. What happened?" Dixie asked, knowing the family would need more answers.

"Her doctors will have better information, but she was unable to clot, which caused her to hemorrhage. She lost a lot of blood but is on the road to a full recovery."

"Thank you, Mom." Dixie squeezed Zane's hand.

"Are you going to introduce me to your friend? Boyfriend?" Her mother inched closer.

"Zane, this is my mother, Dr. Lena Gaynor."

"It's a pleasure." Zane stretched out his arm and shook her mom's hand. "We really appreciate your help."

"Anything for my little pumpkin." She glanced down and frowned. Reaching into Dixie's purse, she pulled out the sandwich. "Really, honey? This is not the way to lose those winter pounds you've been—"

"Excuse us," Zane said. His body tensed, and he squeezed Dixie's hip. "We've been permitted to go see my new niece, and I don't want to miss that opportunity."

"You mean *you* have. I'd liked to have a word with my daughter. Alone," her mother said.

"Not if you're going to talk to her like that." Zane puffed out his chest.

Dixie sucked in a deep breath. "Stop it. Both of you." No way in hell would she stand there and let the man she loved and her fucking mother talk about her as if she weren't even in the room. As if that would help her with her issues. "Zane. I know you mean well, but it's not helping."

He smiled. "I think it did help." He kissed her nose.

"That was backhanded," she whispered. "Mother."

"Don't call me that."

"Then don't call me *pumpkin*. It's rude. And while we're at it, stop telling me what to eat. If you haven't figured it out yet, *you're* part of the problem."

"I am not, and I take offense to that." Her mother planted her hands on her hips. "I've done nothing but try to support you by—"

"Shaming me. That's all you do is fat and food shame me. I'm a grown woman, and I know what putting too much food in my body does to it. And trust me, I work on it every day. But I have triggers, and you're one of them." If Zane wasn't holding her up, she thought she might have fallen over.

Her mother opened her mouth but then snapped it shut. "I'm not going to stand here and be humiliated like this. All I've ever wanted is for you to be healthy." She turned her gaze toward Zane. "If you care about her, I'd think you'd want the same." Her mother turned on her heel and stormed off.

Dixie tried to shake Zane's hold on her hand, but he wouldn't let go.

She tried to push him away, but he wouldn't let her leave his embrace.

"Don't listen to her," he whispered, stroking her hair as he cradled her against his strong chest. "She should be concerned about your happiness *and* your health. The fact she doesn't see that shows how shallow she really is."

Dixie tilted her head.

He wiped the tears from her cheeks.

"You never asked what kind of doctor she is," Dixie said.

"Okay. I'll bite."

"She's a plastic surgeon."

Zane's entire family tried not to laugh, but it proved impossible.

"I'm sorry I pushed your buttons like that, but I couldn't stand seeing how quickly you changed around her," Zane said. "I love you too much to sit back and watch that."

"It's okay. I needed to do that."

"Come on. Let's go meet my niece." He took her by the hand and tugged, only to stop dead in his tracks.

"Hello, Zane," a woman standing in the middle of the corridor said. "I'm surprised to see you with a woman since you prefer dick."

11

Zane swallowed. "Rebecca?"

"In the flesh." She smiled, shrugging her shoulders.

"What the hell are you doing here?"

"You really have to ask?" Rebecca said.

He should have known she'd show up, considering Gayle had introduced him to Rebecca, and they were still friendly—even though Gayle thought Rebecca had been totally wrong when she went to *Page Six* with the story.

Dixie took a step back.

He kept a tight hold of her hand. It was time his secrets came out. "Dixie. This is Rebecca St. Claire."

"The actress," Dixie said softly. "I've seen a few of your movies."

"A fan. How sweet." Rebecca folded her arms and tapped her toe. "I guess you must also know that Zane and I used to be an item."

"I did not… oh." Dixie blinked a few times and looked at Zane. "She's one of your exes?"

"Afraid so," Zane said. "We dated about a year ago."

"Wait. You don't really know about our breakup? You don't read *Page Six*?"

"Don't do this, Rebecca. You're only being vindictive," Zane said.

"That's what happens when you humiliate someone." Rebecca narrowed her eyes.

"You did that all on your own. I'm not the one who sold a bogus story."

Dixie held up her hand. "I don't need to be here for this argument."

"I think you should hear what I have to say." Rebecca aggressively stepped in front of Dixie.

"I'd prefer Zane's side; he'll tell me when he's ready." She smiled at him and nodded.

How he'd so lucked out, he'd never know.

"Brace yourself, girlfriend. Because your lover

will never be able to truly give himself to you because he's in love with someone else."

Dixie laughed. "You are sorely mistaken if you think he's still hung up on you."

"Not me, sweetheart. He never loved me. As a matter of fact, I don't think he can truly love a woman. We're just a distraction while he sits around and waits for his true love."

"Shut up, Rebecca. You don't know what you're talking about." Zane had no idea how to stop Rebecca and the spin she always managed to put on his past love life—or what she *thought* she knew about it.

"If that were true, then why do you want me to keep quiet?" Rebecca tilted her head. "You see, Zane will always be hung up on—"

"This isn't your story to tell," Zane said, the words ground out with a clenched jaw.

"Perhaps not, but since you didn't think to tell me when I was your girlfriend, didn't mention that you were in love with Erik and let me find you in bed with the bouncer of Club Allure, she deserves to know. I mean, it was bad enough I knew the place was evil, but I imagined you fucking some bimbo, not a guy."

"Erik?" Dixie stared at him with her big green

eyes. "The guy who did my interview? That's the man you were in love with?"

Zane blinked. "How do you know I was in love with a man?"

"Not important. You should have told me."

"I know. I planned on it before we got inter-rupted by my mom's phone call to come here," Zane said, letting out a long breath. He rubbed his hands up and down Dixie's arms. "Besides, he's married. And I'm not in love with him. I love you."

"I know that." Dixie shook her head. "I don't care that you were with a man. Or that you loved him in the past. You should know me better than that. My issue is that you cheated on her." She pointed toward Rebecca. "That's not cool."

He let his gaze drop to his feet. No matter how many times he'd defended himself, it always came down to the story Rebecca told. And not the truth. "It's not exactly as it seems."

Dixie poked him in the chest. "You better not ever cheat on me."

"I don't plan on it."

"Oh, for fuck's sake," Rebecca said under her breath. "You two deserve each other." She turned but quickly snapped her focus back to Dixie. "You look familiar," Rebecca said. "I've seen you some-where before."

"I doubt it." Dixie curled her fingers around Zane's biceps. "I need to use the little girls' room."

"Holy shit. You're the chick who writes the *Create the Dew* blog." Rebecca shook her head. "Un-fucking-believable."

"I'm not following," Zane said. "What's *Create the Dew?*"

"No way. You don't know?" Rebecca asked. "Oh, Dixie. Big mistake."

"Just like Erik wasn't your story to tell, neither is this," Dixie said.

"Yeah, but Zane doesn't like his sex life being plastered on the net for the entire world to read about, and that's exactly what you're doing on your blog. You might not have used his name like I did, but once people see you with him, they'll know about your sexual exploits. Like hand jobs in public places or multiple orgasms." Rebecca smiled triumphantly. "I think my work here is done." She turned on her heel and practically skipped down the hallway.

Zane's heart lurched and rose to the back of his throat. He took a step back. "What is she talking about?"

"Something I archived this morning. The thing I was going to tell you about before we found out about—"

"So it's true? You wrote about us having sex and published it on the internet?"

"I took down the two explicit—"

"I don't want to hear it." He raised his hands. "I can't believe you did that to me. To us. To what we had together. Is that all I was to you? Fodder for an article? Is that why you came to the club in the first place? Why you'd rather do that instead of date me when Crystal wanted to fix us up?"

"Will you let me explain?"

"No." He shook his head. "You know how I feel about having my trust betrayed."

"Are you kidding me? You're going to lecture me about trust? You do realize that your *story* doesn't jibe."

"What the hell are you talking about?"

"You told me that you broke up because *she* betrayed your trust. When in reality, *you* cheated on her with your ex-boyfriend."

Zane's jaw dropped open.

"Tell me I'm wrong."

"Rebecca plastered what she *thought* was my indiscretion all over *Page Six*. She nearly ruined

Erik's relationship with his now-husband. She didn't understand that for Erik and me, that last night was our way of saying goodbye to each other. And she has no idea what she really saw. What Rebecca did was make a man feel ugly for being gay."

"Because you didn't inform her of your need to be with Erik and have one last bang before he tied the knot with someone else."

"That's not what happened. You're missing what I'm saying," Zane said. "And I didn't love Rebecca."

Dixie tilted her head. "Do you hear yourself? You can be mad at her all you want for breaking your trust about your sexuality."

"It wasn't about me. She hurt Erik and his husband. And their families. She didn't just put out that she *thought* she caught us in bed together. It went way deeper than that. If you read the article, you'll understand."

"If you'd let me explain my blog, or better yet, read it, you might understand why I did *that*." Dixie dug into her purse and pulled out her cell. "I'll send you everything I wrote and the most recent post. I'll dig up the article on *Page Six*." She swiped at the tear that ran down her cheek. "I'll call a Lyft. Congratulations on being an uncle."

He stood there and watched Dixie walk out of the waiting room.

And out of his life.

Perhaps it was for the best.

Fuck.

His phone vibrated. He stared at a text from Dixie with a link.

To her blog.

He fell back onto one of the metal chairs and tapped the screen. His heart dropped to the pit of his stomach like a cement brick. He loved Dixie. No matter what she'd done, he still loved her.

The question was, could he get past it?

And if he could, would it even matter?

As you can see, I've taken down the posts regarding my sexual relationship. I probably shouldn't even post this, but I promised you, my readers, transparency.

I never told my boyfriend about this blog.

Big mistake.

Huge.

I will be rectifying that today. Tomorrow, when I post, it's possible I could be single, though I'm hopeful that won't be the case. My boyfriend is an amazing man. He's accepted me for exactly who I am, despite my insecurities. In spite of the old tapes that play in my mind that tell me I'm not good enough. Or pretty enough.

Especially the ones that tell me I'm not skinny enough.

Jesus. He hated her mother for putting that into her head. For making her feel as though no man would appreciate her for the loving human being she was, and making her think that all men cared about was a flat stomach.

Which was totally overrated anyway.

My boyfriend has shown me that my size doesn't define me. However, my perception of my size does. And even as I write this, my perception is still skewed. Something I'm constantly working on. But more importantly, he's shown me unconditional love and how I'm deserving of it.

Working as a relationship counselor, I constantly tell my patients to be open and honest with each other. To take risks with their feelings because it's the only way to work through issues.

As I've told you before, it's always easier to advise than to follow advice through in your own life. And for a long time, I wasn't involved in a serious relationship. And when I was, it was with a married man. That's the kind of relationship that will keep any woman in a negative cycle.

I want to be in a healthy, positive partnership, but the only way to do that is to take risks. I thought I was doing that when I first stopped hiding my true identity and then started sharing my intimate thoughts and experiences.

And while it did help me, it's not helping my relationship and only serves to break trust, something I know is very important to my boyfriend.

I will continue writing blog posts regarding sexuality and relationships, but it won't be using my own experiences. It's not fair to those I care about. Of course, tomorrow, I might not have a boyfriend to care about. But that's a risk I have to take. Because if I'm not honest, then I'm not the person he deserves.

Zane held his cell against his chest and stared at the ceiling. He'd experienced her thirst to understand her sexuality firsthand and knew how her weight and her perception of her body held her back. He'd also learned a lot about himself through their shared encounters.

Mostly, he'd fallen in love with the most amazing woman he'd ever met.

"There you are," Xavier said as he plopped down on the chair adjacent to Zane's. "I just ran into Rebecca. I can't believe she's here. Gayle asked her to leave out of respect for our family. Hopefully, you won't run into her."

"Too late," Zane said. "And she caused a bit of a scene with Dixie."

"Shit. Where is Dixie?"

"I fucked up, Xavier. I fucked up good this time."

12

"Thanks for coming." Dixie pulled open the door and let in the tall, dark, and handsome bouncer she'd met at Club Allure.

"I wasn't going to," Erik said.

"What changed your mind?" Dixie waved him into her family room, where he took a seat on the sofa.

"Honestly? Seeing Zane mope around the club these past few days."

It had been three days since she'd last seen Zane.

He hadn't texted.

Or called.

That spoke volumes.

After reading the article that Rebecca had submitted to *Page Six*, Dixie understood why Zane would be pissed. Rebecca had made Zane out to be a home-wrecker—which he wasn't.

She'd painted Zane as a sexual predator. A man who exploited both men and women.

Nothing could be further from the truth.

She'd also planted lie after lie about him and his family.

And a few about Erik.

Dixie was amazed that Zane hadn't sued her for slander or something.

Page Six actually wrote a retraction to the article, but it didn't matter. The damage had been done, and the world felt sorry for Rebecca.

"I haven't heard from him since Lilly was born," she admitted.

"Zane can be his own worst enemy sometimes." Erik fiddled with his wedding ring, a habit she'd noticed the first night she met him. "He's a proud man who doesn't like his privacy stripped from him."

"I noticed. And I shouldn't have used our sex life as blog material."

"You didn't know the two of you would fall in love with each other."

She let out a short laugh. "This is true. But still. Before I wrote the second blog post, he'd told me that some girl had betrayed his trust. He just hadn't given me the details."

"He's still trying to protect me."

"What do you mean?"

"It's complicated."

"Enlighten me," she said.

"My family didn't know I was gay. The article in *Page Six* outed me. My family hasn't spoken to me since."

"I'm so sorry."

He shrugged. "They needed to know the truth about me. However, Zane has always felt responsible for causing my family to cut all ties. But it's not his fault. It's theirs. Now, what do you really want to know?"

"Did Rebecca catch you and Zane having sex? Because after thinking about what Zane said to me the other day, reading the article, and talking with some people, I don't believe she caught the two of you fucking."

Erik smiled. "Zane was right about you being smart."

"If you weren't having sex, then why did both of you let her perpetuate the story?"

"Once the story broke, my husband—then-boyfriend—had to answer a lot of questions from his family. While they all knew about his gayness, they didn't know about me. They thought he was still with someone else. Someone they loved and never wanted to see him break up with. So that came as a shock."

"Jesus. I'm sorry. This sounds like a shitshow," she said. "Did the other guy—?"

"Oh. They were long broken up." Erik held up his hand. "But between his family and mine, we realized all the secrets and lies were only killing us. In a way, Rebecca did us all a favor. But Zane still can't see it that way."

"Why not?"

Erik tapped the center of his chest. "Her intentions weren't pure. She had malice in her heart. All Rebecca wanted to do was hurt everyone involved, and Zane took that personally." Erik leaned forward, resting his elbows on his knees. "He'd be pissed at me for being here. And more upset for me saying this, but since he can't get his head out of his ass, someone has to do it. Zane is one of the sweetest men I know. Some people would call him an empath. So, when people he cares about are in pain, he hurts, too. It was easier for him to take the fall than to force her to come out and tell the truth because he wanted my husband and me to be happy."

Dixie swallowed the lump in her throat. "That does sound like Zane."

"He printed out your blog and the ones you archived that you sent him. He reads them every day. All day. Your words are genuine. You write with heart and the kind of vulnerability that helps people. Not hurts them. While you might have shared a sexual experience, you did so in a way that empowers women. And men. I think Zane feels as though he's stifled you somehow and hates himself for it. The same way he took responsibility for what happened with Rebecca."

"You think he's mad that I took down the blog and am writing on more clinical topics?"

"It's not that he wants you to write about your sex life with him. But rather the way you came to understand how your perception of yourself hadn't come full circle yet. And how you managed to embrace your sexuality in new ways." Erik stood. "I know what it's like to be loved by Zane. And that man loves you with every fiber of his being. He'll come around, but do you really want to wait for him to stop sulking? Because, trust me, he can do it for weeks." Erik bent and kissed her cheek. "I'll see myself out."

Tomorrow.

She'd go see Zane tomorrow.

Dixie poured herself a glass of wine and made herself a tray of cheese and crackers. It was a nice night; she'd enjoy a quiet evening by the water.

She sucked in a deep, cleansing breath as she made her way down to the dock. She rolled up her jeans and dipped her feet into the cool water. The sunrays burned through the thick Seattle haze.

Leaning back, she gently kicked her feet, splashing.

The wood planks rattled.

She glanced over her shoulder.

Zane.

The air in her lungs flew out like a rocket racing to the moon.

"What are you doing here?" she asked.

He sat down next to her and took a big swig of her wine. "I should ask *you* what Erik was doing here, but he already told me."

"I see." She stared at the ripples in the water. "Are you mad?"

"No. I understand you just wanted to hear his side of things, but you could have asked me."

"You haven't been talking to me," she said.

"That's a two-way street."

"Good point," she said. "I needed some time and space. I wasn't sure I could think rationally about anything between what happened with my mother and then Rebecca."

He reached out and tucked her hair behind her ear. "What are you thinking now?"

"That we're both slightly wounded when it comes to love, and we tried to protect ourselves but ended up hurting each other instead."

"I'm sorry, Dixie. I overreacted when Rebecca brought up your blog. I should have at least listened to you."

"I shouldn't have written the posts without your permission."

He palmed her cheek. "I don't know about that. I've read and reread them a dozen times. They're so beautiful, and I love how you express yourself and how it helps people. I don't want to take that from you."

"You're not."

"I'm still reading your blog, and the tone has changed. I hate that."

"I think I'm still helping my readers."

"Maybe," he said. "But it's not the same. I mean, if what you felt with me, and what has happened between us since, can help other couples —or women who struggle with feeling good about themselves—then I want to be a part of that." He ran his hand through his hair. "You haven't even asked me why I didn't tell you about Erik."

"Why didn't you?"

"I wasn't sure how you'd feel about me being bisexual or the fact that the only other person I've ever loved was a man. People judge you for being overweight. Well, I get the same judgments. But you're not like that. Nor am I. And I don't want to be the man who stops you from doing what you're passionate about."

"You'd really be okay if I put what happened between us in the beginning back up? The entire blog? And write more?"

"Yes, I would. I am. I only ask that, going forward, the specific details of our sex life stay private. Unless you discuss it with me and let me read it first. But the emotions… The growth. How women deal with their sexuality. Weight. Self-perceptions. All that, you need to write it. And you need to do it from the heart." He tapped the center of her chest. "I love you, Dixie. I don't want to be the person who prevents you from being you. I want to be the man who supports you and stands by you."

She swiped the tear that escaped her eye. "Can I put that in my blog?"

He laughed. "Only if you tell me you still love me."

"I might have to think about that." She flung her arms around his body, only she did so a little too aggressively.

Splash!

The chilly water clung to her clothes. She kicked her feet and swiped her wet hair from her face. She popped up from the water and looked around.

Zane shook his head like a wet dog. "Are you okay?" He pulled her to the dock.

"Just cold and drippy."

"You and me both." He jumped up onto the wooden planks and offered her a hand but then yanked it back.

"Hey."

"No help from me until I hear the words."

"That's a little childish, don't you think?" She took her hand and smacked it against the surface of the water, splashing his face.

"No more than what you just did." He wrung out some of his hair.

She smiled. "You're a big pain in the ass. But I love you anyway. Now help me up." She took his hand.

And yanked.

"Oh, you're——" He fell into the water wearing a grin. He popped back up and shook his head. "…in big trouble."

She wrapped her arms around his shoulders. "You're the only sweet temptation I'll ever need."

He took her mouth in a slow, hot kiss. In that moment, she knew she was right where she belonged. She'd found her forever, and here in his arms is where she'd stay.

Thank you for reading FLIRT AWAY. Next in the series is PRODUCE AWAY. Please feel free to leave an honest review!

Grab a glass of vino, kick back, relax, and let the romance roll in…

Sign up for my Newsletter (https://dl.bookfunnel.com/

82gm8b9k4y) where I often give away free books before publication.

Join my private Facebook group (https://www.facebook.com/groups/191706547909047/) where I post exclusive excerpts and discuss all things murder and love!

ABOUT THE AUTHOR

Jen Talty is the *USA Today* Bestselling Author of Contemporary Romance, Romantic Suspense, and Paranormal Romance. In the fall of 2020, her short story was selected and featured in a 1001 Dark Nights Anthology.

Regardless of the genre, her goal is to take you on a ride that will leave you floating under the sun with warmth in your heart. She writes stories about broken heroes and heroines who aren't necessarily looking for romance, but in the end, they find the kind of love books are written about :).

She first started writing while carting her kids to one hockey rink after the other, averaging 170 games per year between 3 kids in 2 countries and 5 states. Her first book, IN TWO WEEKS was originally published in 2007. In 2010 she helped form a publishing company (Cool Gus Publishing) with *NY*

Times Bestselling Author Bob Mayer where she ran the technical side of the business through 2016.

Jen is currently enjoying the next phase of her life…the empty nester! She and her husband reside in Jupiter, Florida.

Grab a glass of vino, kick back, relax, and let the romance roll in…

Sign up for my Newsletter (https://dl.bookfunnel.com/82gm8b9k4y) where I often give away free books before publication.

Join my private Facebook group (https://www.facebook.com/groups/191706547909047/) where I post exclusive excerpts and discuss all things murder and love!

Never miss a new release. Follow me on Amazon:amazon.com/author/jentalty

And on Bookbub: bookbub.com/authors/jen-talty

ALSO BY JEN TALTY

Brand new series: SAFE HARBOR!

MINE TO KEEP

MINE TO SAVE

MINE TO PROTECT

Check out LOVE IN THE ADIRONDACKS!

SHATTERED DREAMS

AN INCONVENIENT FLAME

THE WEDDING DRIVER

CLEAR BLUE SKY

NY STATE TROOPER SERIES (also set in the Adirondacks!)

In Two Weeks

Dark Water

Deadly Secrets

Murder in Paradise Bay

To Protect His own

Deadly Seduction

When A Stranger Calls

His Deadly Past

The Corkscrew Killer

Brand New Novella for the First Responders series

A spin-off from the NY State Troopers series

PLAYING WITH FIRE

PRIVATE CONVERSATION

THE RIGHT GROOM

AFTER THE FIRE

CAUGHT IN THE FLAMES

CHASING THE FIRE

Legacy Series

Dark Legacy

Legacy of Lies

Secret Legacy

Emerald City

INVESTIGATE AWAY

SAIL AWAY

Colorado Brotherhood Protectors

Fighting For Esme

Defending Raven

Fay's Six

Yellowstone Brotherhood Protectors

Guarding Payton

Candlewood Falls

RIVERS EDGE

THE BURIED SECRET

ITS IN HIS KISS

LIPS OF AN ANGEL

It's all in the Whiskey

JOHNNIE WALKER

GEORGIA MOON

JACK DANIELS

JIM BEAM

WHISKEY SOUR

WHISKEY COBBLER

WHISKEY SMASH

IRISH WHISKEY

The Monroes

COLOR ME YOURS

COLOR ME SMART

COLOR ME FREE

COLOR ME LUCKY

COLOR ME ICE

COLOR ME HOME

Search and Rescue

PROTECTING AINSLEY

PROTECTING CLOVER

PROTECTING OLYMPIA

PROTECTING FREEDOM

PROTECTING PRINCESS

PROTECTING MARLOWE

DELTA FORCE-NEXT GENERATION

SHIELDING JOLENE

SHIELDING AALYIAH

SHIELDING LAINE

SHIELDING TALULLAH

SHIELDING MARIBEL

The Men of Thief Lake

REKINDLED

DESTINY'S DREAM

Federal Investigators

JANE DOE'S RETURN

THE BUTTERFLY MURDERS

THE AEGIS NETWORK

The Sarich Brother

THE LIGHTHOUSE

HER LAST HOPE

THE LAST FLIGHT

THE RETURN HOME

THE MATRIARCH

More Aegis Network

MAX & MILIAN

A CHRISTMAS MIRACLE

SPINNING WHEELS

HOLIDAY'S VACATION

Special Forces Operation Alpha

BURNING DESIRE

BURNING KISS

BURNING SKIES

BURNING LIES

BURNING HEART

BURNING BED

REMEMBER ME ALWAYS

The Brotherhood Protectors

Out of the Wild

ROUGH JUSTICE

ROUGH AROUND THE EDGES

ROUGH RIDE

ROUGH EDGE

ROUGH BEAUTY

The Brotherhood Protectors

The Saving Series

SAVING LOVE

SAVING MAGNOLIA

SAVING LEATHER

Hot Hunks

Cove's Blind Date Blows Up

My Everyday Hero – Ledger

Tempting Tavor

Malachi's Mystic Assignment

Needing Neor

Holiday Romances

A CHRISTMAS GETAWAY

ALASKAN CHRISTMAS

WHISPERS

CHRISTMAS IN THE SAND

Heroes & Heroines on the Field

TAKING A RISK

TEE TIME

A New Dawn

THE BLIND DATE

SPRING FLING

SUMMERS GONE

WINTER WEDDING

THE AWAKENING

The Collective Order

THE LOST SISTER

THE LOST SOLDIER

THE LOST SOUL

THE LOST CONNECTION

THE NEW ORDER

www.ingramcontent.com/pod-product-compliance
Lightning Source LLC
Chambersburg PA
CBHW070656100726
47907CB00007B/2224